Inside Sam Lerner

Inside Sam Lerner

Gwen Banta

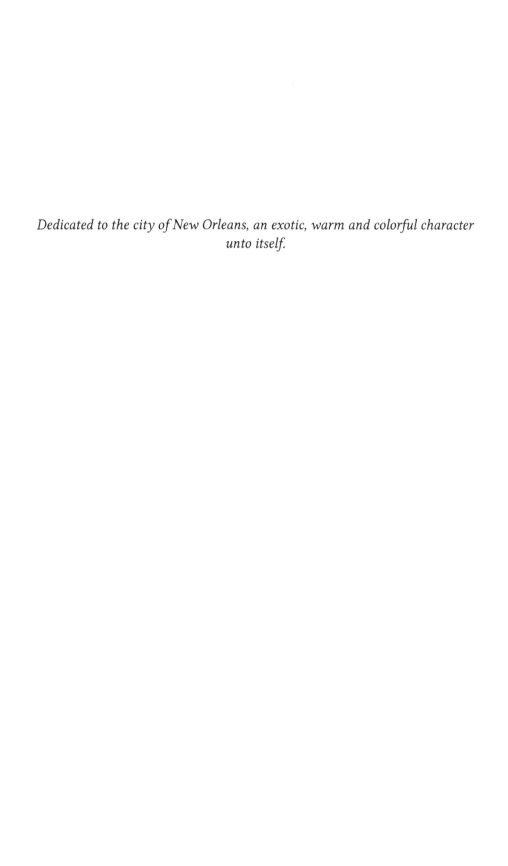

Dedicated to the city of New Orleans, an exotic, warm and colorful character unto itself.

Chapter 1

Sam couldn't stop staring at the clerk's ears. The holes in the kid's lobes were big enough to accommodate corks, and indeed, they did. The laconic young man had also pushed the limits of self-expression by having himself tattooed like a road map. Sam was sure that if he looked at the kid's body art long enough he'd find an arrow and the words YOU ARE HERE.

"Cash only," the clerk drawled, flicking his studded tongue over his crooked lower lip.

Sam winced. He was wondering if he had made a wrong turn on his way south to New Orleans and was still stuck in Los Angeles. After he tossed down the money for the two six-packs, he hustled out of the road stop off old Route 434. While yanking the tab off a brew, he analyzed the differences he'd discovered since he pulled into St. Tammany Parish, Louisiana, under a tarp of heat and dust.

He had taken a detour to the old abandoned family home, but to his surprise, the house had vanished. Gone was the home where Sam had learned to piss and hit his mark, where he had hidden Willie Mays trading cards behind the baseboards, and where he had set his room on fire while distilling homemade brew at the age of ten. The place had been leveled, with nothing more than a weed headstone left in memory of his earliest years.

Sam kicked a rock out of his pathway and wondered how Dorothy would have felt if she had returned to Kansas to discover nothing but a parking lot. Some things are just not supposed to change, he groused to himself.

Sam plopped down on an overstuffed chair outside the road stop, slung one booted foot over its tattered arm, and chugged until he had to stop for breath.

He knew it was time to push on across Lake Ponchartrain to the Big Easy, but not without dulling a few painful memories first.

He was just popping another Dixie when he saw a police car pull off the highway onto the dirt turnaround outside the road stop. The unforgiving June sun was high in the sky, obliterating his view of the driver. But it didn't matter: a cop was a cop.

Avoiding the cop's direct gaze, Sam pretended to adjust his pant leg while pulling a jack knife out of one stained boot. After flicking the knife open, he made a half-hearted attempt to scrape the coating of caked mud off his heel. He kept his eyes averted and his keen ears alert while the heavy footsteps approached. Sweat retreated down his neck into his chest hairs. When the tips of the officer's black shoes stopped just short of his own, he became very still, resigning himself to an unwelcome encounter. Sam Lerner was in no mood to be civil.

"You're not drinkin' and drivin,' are ya?" the deep voice drawled at him.

"Do I look like I'm driving?" Sam continued to work his boot as if it were a complicated physics problem. As he kept his head down, he expertly sized up the cop by the length of his shoes. Sam had learned avoidance of confrontation early in life. It was later in his mercurial life that he had learned to relish it. Today, he knew he could go either way. *Get the fuck out of my face,* his silent voice warned his unwelcome guest.

"That your Shelby Cobra parked there?"

"Yes it is. Is there a problem, officer?"

"Only if you continue to dissect that boot without passin' me a beer. It's hotter than a whorehouse pussy out here."

Sam breathed in the dust and resigned himself to the fact that there was no way to avoid being pleasant. Not this time. Not this cop. He mustered up about as much congeniality as he had been able to find in recent days. "Sit your fat ass down, shitbag," he growled, popping another brew.

"Sam, my man, that's no way to talk to an esteemed officer of the law," the cop laughed, "especially an old pal."

"Depends on who's doin' the esteemin', Duval. Figured I'd run into you sooner or later. 'Was hopin' for later. I'm not in the mood for cordiality, but I guess I've got no choice. How the hell you been all these years?" he asked offering a handshake.

"Better than you, I take it." Duval clutched Sam's hand in one large bear claw while he placed his other hand on Sam's shoulder.

"Yep, 'imagine so. But it's good to be back. Congratulations, Duval, I hear you bought yourself Captain's rank, complete with matching decoder ring. No offense of course."

"No offense taken. And you look like shit, Sammy boy–offense intended."

"That's part of your charm, Duval." Sam allowed the words to drift from his mouth like smoke rings.

Duval shot him a cheesy grin. "Aw, you're still good-looking – a goddamn pussy magnet, you sonuvabitch. You been out knockin' around the old burg?" He dragged over an old rocker while waiting for an answer.

As Sam waited for him to sit, he marveled at how the lug still lowered himself into a chair as if he were about to take a crap. Leon Duval was huge, even sitting. Four decades had passed since they had met as kids, and almost two since they had last seen each other; and Duval was still big, still soft, and still grinning.

"Sorry I'm crabby, buddy. I haven't slept much the past week," Sam offered as a way of explaining his unkempt appearance and lack of civility. He smiled back out of force of habit. "After driving from Los Angeles, I took a detour out to the old homestead, which I discovered was history. I guess nothing stays the same."

"Pisser, huh? There was a fire out there a while back, but the St. Tammany Fire Department just jacked-off while the old shacks burned. I think they figured there was nothing worth endangering themselves for. Prob'ly right. That place never had much to offer us, Sammy."

"Perhaps. So what are you doing this far out of your jurisdiction?" Sam aimed a finger gun at the New Orleans Police Department seal on Duval's car and pulled the trigger.

"I knew you were coming, pal. I've kept track of you over the years. Everybody down here read about you being head dick in that case where that famous rapper got the death sentence. Hell, I even saw you on the tube–you're a frickin' hero!"

"Tell that to the rapper's homeboys."

"Yeah, I bet they'd like a piece of you. Anyway, I've got a friend in L.A.P.D. who said you'd gone and bailed out of LaLa land and were headin' this way. I've been keeping tabs since I heard you stopped by Fred's Lounge in Mamou for a little Cajun music on the way into town. That car is easy to spot. If I'd known sooner, I would have joined you. I wanted to give you a proper welcome home, one old teammate to another."

"Is that right?" Sam cocked his head to study Duval.

"Yup, I'm proud of you, buddy. I hear you were one of the Jeffersons up there in the land of fruits and nuts."

"Huh?"

"Jefferson." At Sam's blank stare, Duval tapped one toe and began to sing, " 'Movin' on up, to the East side…'"

"Oh," Sam groaned, "*George* Jefferson. For chrissake, you watch too many re-runs."

Duval shrugged. "Guess so. My wife Linny left me," he then announced in a complete non sequitur. "Not because of the TV thing, though."

"Sorry to hear that."

"Yeah. Anyway, I wanted to say welcome."

"Thanks. Can I go now?" Sam flicked his knife closed, shoved it back into his boot, and stood up to leave.

"Still Mr. Charming, I see." Duval stopped Sam with one bear paw while grabbing a Dixie with the other. "Thanks, I'm sure ya don't mind if I help myself, seein' as how I'm off-duty. You gonna shack up at Maire's Gentlemen's Club when you hit the Quarter?"

"I thought about it."

"Well, stay out of trouble."

"Yes, sir, Officer, sir," Sam responded dutifully.

"You okay to drive? I'm told that you and the booze wagon have a sporadic relationship."

"That's describes all my relationships. And tell your L.A. copper friend he talks too much."

"I asked him about you outta concern, you know."

Sam looked at Duval's contrite face and felt guilty for snarling. Then he felt pissed for feeling guilty. Duval was always getting him all jammed up. "Thanks for your concern, but I'm in a holding pattern of a few brews a day now."

"Yeah, I don't blame ya. I heard about your wife dying and all. Terrible thing. I'm really sorry, buddy."

"That makes two of us." Sam threw the six-packs into the back of the Shelby and jumped in. Beatrice, his Golden Retriever, opened one eye long enough to make sure it was him. After she yawned, she went back to sleep. "You're a helluva security system, Beatrice," Sam muttered.

"Sweet pup," Duval said, checking out the car as he leaned in the driver's window. "And the old Shelby is lookin' mighty sweet herself. Glad to see you still have her."

"Yeah, at least this girl won't die on me." His words were sharper than he intended. "You know—good engine and all," he quickly added, forcing his feelings back down into the emotional box he kept wedged in his chest.

Duval reached out to shake Sam's hand. "Well, welcome home. And don't get into any trouble over at Maire's. I'd hate to arrest a Los Angeles cop in an escort establishment. I hear you guys are lethal."

"Ex-cop," Sam corrected him as he fired up the Shelby, "but I'm still lethal." He grabbed a beer from the back, propped it between his knees, and pulled the tab. Then Sam stepped on the gas, enjoying both the surge of power and the numbing effects of the alcohol as he screeched down the highway to New Orleans, completely unaware that he was heading into an abyss far worse than the one he had left behind.

Chapter 2

Sam drove at an easy pace, allowing the lull of the Shelby engine to ease his agitation. He had purchased the car after saving enough money working summers and after school with Leon Duval at St. Tammany's mortuary, which had proven to be good preparation for their future careers. Perhaps it had been more than coincidence that both Sam and Duval had become homicide detectives, for both had long ago learned to disassociate themselves from the macabre parade of deads they administered to on a daily basis.

After college, Duval made a somewhat dubious name for himself in the New Orleans Police Department while Sam headed for Los Angeles with dreams of fishing, surfing, and sun-tanned blondes. Instead Sam encountered race riots, quakes, and graft. Nonetheless he made it to the top of the detective pile, gathering a fistful of commendations along the way. Sam was one of the best L.A.P.D. had to offer, and he put his job ahead of all else in his life, until he met Kira.

Sam instinctively shoved his wife's image from his memory. It was still too painful to imagine her smile. After nine years of a great marriage, she was now gone. Just like that–gone forever. Now California was dead to him, too.

Only one week had passed since he had finally decided to bail out of L.A. and not look back…not that he could see too straight these days anyway. Since Kira's death, he had discovered that inebriation was quite underrated as a form of therapy.

Sam gave the Shelby a bit more gas just to feel her respond–an assurance to himself that something still could. Over the years he had brought the car back to cherry condition. He knew it was time to do the same for himself.

Maybe tomorrow, he silently thought as he watched Beatrice muster up the energy to climb into the front seat to beg for a sip of Dixie. "Easy girl," Sam cautioned, "I'll need to see some I.D."

He was never sure if his conversations with his dog were for her benefit or his. Either way, his own voice helped fill the void Kira's death had left in his life.

Beatrice licked his hand, belched, then hung her head out the window. "Couldn't have said it better myself, girl," Sam grinned.

As Sam appraised the scenery, he recalled how St. Tammany had been another ending. And he was tired of endings. The house he had once lived in had been nothing more than a four room clapboard bungalow, but he and his father and Mammy Jem had lived there until he was a teen. It was home, as much as any place had ever been. Now the house was a memory, just like the old man, whose gin-marinated corpse lay in a crypt somewhere near the French Quarter. Jem had not written to him for two years, her old eyes a bit too thick with cataracts to relish correspondence.

Ah, Jem... she was someone Sam could smell if he put his mind to it–sweat mixed with exotic spices, rum, and wood smoke. Her strong Creole hands had consoled him as a boy, stroking his head until he could allow himself to fall asleep.

Sleep had never come easily for Sam, not since the hurricane had roared through town with its high winds hurling debris like exploding railroad cars. He mostly remembered the noise and the echo of his father's screams as he pulled Sam's mother out from beneath the heavy religious triptych that had hung over their bed.

Sam soon came to understand the bitter irony of that night. In his young mind, his mother had been murdered by Jesus. Yep, Jesus was the perp, he had told himself, and the heavy crucifix was the weapon. Now Sam cocked a brow as he recalled his first great detective work.

Jem had stayed on as his mammy; and she was truly the only mother he remembered. Sam took another swig as he tried to recall Jem's real name. He couldn't. He had nicknamed her Jemima when he was four years old, enthralled by her resemblance to the mammy on the pancake box with the same name. Now he shook his head at his youthful lack of political correctness, but Jem had always professed to love the name. That's because she loved Sam.

The memories of Jem allowed him to ease back into his seat even more. Perhaps he would see her tomorrow. Tonight, however, he was going to enjoy the comfort of a different kind of woman. Sam smiled as he goosed the Shelby. At last he was returning to the city he loved. And to the one other person in his life that was still there for him.

* * *

Sam's heart was racing faster than the Shelby as he crossed Lake Ponchartrain into New Orleans. He grinned unconsciously as he sucked in the familiar scent of lake water mingled with the dense fragrance of the Mississippi River. In the distance, the wail of a river boat horn seeped out from under the oppressive humidity.

He took in the lights of the beckoning town and studied her undulating skyline. The old city still excited him. Even Beatrice was alert, somehow sensing the change in his mood. The sun was creeping down over the smoldering town as the night began to come to life.

Sam headed straight for the French Quarter, already teaming with revelers despite the lingering summer heat. As he settled into the familiarity of his surroundings, he switched on the radio and heard the vibrant sounds of Chubby Carrier's *Zydeco Junkie*. He had missed the Creole music reminiscent of his childhood. The Cajun dialect and fast tempo always infused him with an excitement he had never been able to describe to his friends back in Los Angeles who had grown up with surfing and the Beach Boys.

A grin spread across his tan face he passed a sidewalk sandwich board that advertised "Beer So Cold You Will Slap Your Mama." Weaving through the Quarter, he passed rows of gable-sided Creole cottages, his focus lingering on a colorful pink cottage sporting lime shutters and displaying a For Sale sign in the courtyard. The rider on the sign proudly announced, 'Haunted.' Jem had always said New Orleans was a town that did everything with a flourish and a wink. The ol' girl was right.

When he arrived at the corner of St. Claude and Ursulines, Sam parked on the street and stared at a stately guest house known as Maire's Gentlemen's Club. A soft pink glow backlit the windows, and the sound of Fats Waller clung to the thick air like the smell of sex. "Christ," he whispered, "I'm back." He briefly looked away, knowing if he took it all in at once he'd have to deal with emotions better left undisturbed.

After letting Beatrice sniff around long enough to make her mark in the Quarter, he left her in the Shelby and tentatively approached the door of the guest house. He had to ring several times before someone finally answered.

The carved door opened so quietly it hardly displaced the fragrant air that covered Sam like a familiar old sweater. His senses were so weighted with anticipation it seemed the world had gone into slow motion.

Suddenly she was there, all six feet of her, as elegant as she had always been, and draped in pink silk. Maire Girod was a unique combination of green eyes, tawny skin and close-cropped blond hair that was nappy and coarse–a result of her African, French and Canadian heritage. She was as beautiful to him now as she was the first moment they had met when he was only sixteen. "Maire," he whispered.

Maire stared for a moment, and then she wrapped herself around him, enveloping him in a warm cloud of jasmine. He held her tightly while his breath slowly found an escape.

"Chere," she whispered in soft Cajun tones, "we've been waiting for you. It's been a long time."

"It *has* been a long time," he smiled as he kissed her cheek. Sam then pulled back to stare at her angular face and creamy skin which was nearly flawless, except for the light lines etched by time at the corners of her eyes. "And you're still breathtaking."

"And you are still my handsome cowboy," she smiled as she led him by the hand into the parlor, which was full of fresh flowers from the courtyard garden.

Sam noticed with pleasure that all of the furniture was the same. The antique rose brocade chaises and sofas and the silk lamp shades were barely faded. Gold framed mirrors reflected the soft parlor light. He had long ago committed the details to memory.

As Maire sat on the sofa and pulled him down next to her, he was overwhelmed once more. He cleared his throat while she reached for the bottle of cognac on the coffee table. "Drink this, love," she said as she poured the amber liquid into a glass. "This is indeed a moment worth toasting."

"Thanks, Maire. So how did you know I was coming?"

Her sly grin revealed a perfect set of teeth. "Someone who runs an honorable establishment like mine always knows when a man is 'coming.' It's simply good business."

Sam laughed and sipped his drink. As he leaned back into the couch, he was aware that it had been too long since he had felt safe enough to let down his guard.

Maire studied his face like a painting as she answered his question. "Leon Duval was here last night."

"I should have known. I ran into him over near the old place in St Tammany on my way here. He's still annoying, and I suspect he's still as crooked as they come."

"I can't deny that. But he means well, chere. He's just a bit overbearing. He still looks up to you like he did back in school."

"Well now I feel guilty as hell."

Maire laughed and intertwined her long fingers in his. "Don't feel guilty. Leon Duval *is* annoying. He told me what happened back in Los Angeles–to Kira I mean. I'm truly sorry, chere. I'm glad you decided to come back home awhile though. Oh, Antoine wants you to drop by Tujagues while you're in town. He has been expecting you."

"Antoine's expecting me, too? Christ, did Duval take up skywriting or something?"

"Never mind about Duval. Are you okay, Sam?"

"Not really. But I'm feeling better by the second."

"You need some sleep," she soothed as she reached out to rub his temples. When she rang a bell on the coffee table, a young blonde in her late twenties with a full, sensuous body stepped into the room. After she eyed Sam, she flashed a seductive smile.

Maire held up a hand in warning. "Sorry, Celeste, but this one is off-limits. Please offer hors d'oeuvres to the gentlemen in the garden, and then send in Madsen."

Celeste shot them a look of disappointment. As she dutifully opened the door to the courtyard and stepped out, Sam got a glimpse of several male callers laughing near the fountain. Celeste eyed Sam hungrily before she closed the door and disappeared into the warm evening.

"We seldom have guests as ruggedly appealing as you are, Sam," Maire smiled, explaining Celeste's disappointment.

"You still know how to make a man feel special. No wonder business is good."

"You *are* special. I want you to take the room in the back. Coffee and beignets at sun-up. We'll catch up then."

"Are you coming up with me?"

"You know a hostess never leaves the party. But, darlin,' you sure make a girl think twice."

"I've been waiting since I was sixteen," he teased.

"That's back when I was an old lady of twenty-one. I'm ancient now, so I'm only being merciful. I'll send in Madsen. I told her to expect you."

"Apparently everybody has been awaiting my arrival. I get more press than the Pope."

"You're more important, so no charge for you. *He'd* have to pay."

"That's why you're a successful businesswoman. Speaking of charge, Maire. I have another girl in my charge. She's in the car. May I bring her in?"

"You getting kinky in your old age?"

"I'm not getting anything in my old age."

She shook her head as she traced his square jaw with a delicate finger. "Such a loss. Show her in, chere."

When Sam opened the door and whistled, Beatrice sat up, jumped out the car window, and ran for the veranda. Maire let out a sultry chuckle before leading Sam and Beatrice up the curved staircase to the one place where he could still find comfort.

* * *

Sam stepped out of the shower off Madsen's room, grateful to be somewhere familiar. Beatrice, who had crawled under an altar set with religious offerings, was eyeing a voodoo rattle-doll somewhat suspiciously. Sam remembered only enough of Mammy Jem's teachings to recognize a veve symbol that was painted on the wall, and a small table with divination cards that was set up in one corner. As accustomed as he was to Jem's voodoo practices while growing up, Sam still found the various objects and idols very foreign. But tonight he was too exhausted to give them a second glance.

The full length shuttered windows were open, allowing bits of conversation, blues rifts and laughter to drift his way from the garden below. On the ceiling above his head, a fan turned slowly, folding the sounds and fragrances into the night air.

When Sam peered down into the courtyard below, one patron, obscured by fingers of shade from a large magnolia tree, looked up at him and nod-ded. Blonde Celeste, who was now outstretched seductively on a wrought iron lounge, followed the man's gaze. When she spotted Sam, she languorously adjusted her pose then stroked her pale legs, pausing to circle the fleur de lis tattoo on her calf with a red long fingernail. The patron cordially lifted a glass to Sam before continuing his social call with Celeste.

Sam closed the shutters and glanced around. He was already forming a profile of the young woman who inhabited the comfortable room. After years of detective work, he was the master of the fifteen-second profile. This Madsen was a loner he figured–no family photos or memorabilia. On her vanity there were several scarves, various ropes of plastic carnival beads, and a plastic baby Jesus from a Mardi Gras King Cake.

She also owned several hair brushes, including a brush with a bone handle that had been repaired with glue. Next to the brush was a bottle of fragrance–Dolce & Gabbana Velvet Desire, which he recognized as an expensive designer brand. A wooden fruit bowl with a lone fruit fly feasting on a bruised peach completed the arrangement.

It was the tiny stuffed canaries in the room, however, that held Sam's eye. Madsen had strategically placed lifelike pairs of yellow canaries everywhere. The birds stared at Sam curiously as he walked about. One pair was perched next to a little plate of sesame seeds, and several were nestled in plants. Sam figured the girl was either superstitious, or perhaps very lonely. However, his experiences in homicide had revealed more peculiar interests than a collection of stuffed canaries.

Reminding himself that he was no longer a detective, Sam finally crawled between the sheets and reached for the chime. A few moments later he heard the knock.

"Come in, chere," he said, unconsciously slipping back into the Cajun dialect he had worked so long to lose.

Madsen stepped into the room. She was young–twenty-two at most he'd guess. Her skin reminded him of buttered toast, and her eyes tilted upward in a small face accented by full lips. A fuchsia and yellow colored chiffon scarf was tied at the waistline of her strapless black dress; and she had chosen lipstick to match the pink of the scarf. Sam smiled with pleasure. He loved to look at beautiful things; and to him, all women were beautiful.

"Sam Lerner?" she said softly. As he nodded his head, her tentative smile grew larger. "Would you like to talk for a while. Maybe about California?" The expectant look on her face was almost childlike.

"I don't think so, thank you. I'm exhausted–I've been on the road a long while."

"You've had plenty to eat?"

"No appetite."

"Would you enjoy a libation?" she offered.

"I've had a libation, thank you, Madsen." Sam smiled at the word, which she had mispronounced. She was delightful, and very small town–just the way he had been on his first solo trip into New Orleans as a sixteen-year-old looking to become a man. In some respects, he figured, he was still trying to become one.

"Would you like me to join you for a libation, Madsen?" he asked, remembering his manners.

"No, thank you, I don't drink. Is your dog friendly?"

"If she were any sweeter she'd need insulin."

Madsen giggled before she methodically began to undress, humming unconsciously as she hung each garment. The only thing Madsen did not remove was an oblong silver pendant, which was hanging from a long chain around her neck. She slipped into a chenille robe and tied it at her waist, still humming.

Sam closed his eyes and listened. Her voice was so damn sweet it made him ache. When she moved closer, he noticed that her scent was sweet also, like wet flowers.

"Maire told me what you need," she whispered as she crawled into bed, keeping her robe wrapped around her. "You're sure this is all you want, Mr. Lerner?"

"I'm sure, darling." Sam's breathing grew deep and steady. The notes of Louis Armstrong's version of *La Vie En Rose* drifted up from the garden, slowing forcing his pain to loosen its tenacious grip from his chest.

Madsen lifted her hand to stroke Sam's forehead. "You have pretty blue eyes."

"Thank you, Madsen."

"I like blue eyes with black hair. I wish I had that."

"You're perfect just the way you are," he assured her.

"That's very kind of you."

Sam made an unsuccessful attempt to continue the conversation, but his exhaustion was pressing him deeper into the soft down pillow.

"Shhh." Madsen traced her fingers down his face and caressed his lips with the back of her hand. Using her finger tips, she gently applied pressure above Sam's brow, pausing occasionally to smooth the hair back from his forehead.

Her hands were soft and nurturing, allowing him to drift to some safe place from long ago.

As his body sunk into a long-forgotten state of calm, he felt her fingertips brush away the moisture from his cheek. He had allowed his long-suppressed sadness to surface, but he was too tired to give a damn. He just wanted someone near him so he could finally sleep.

Unfortunately, it would be the last good sleep Sam Lerner would have for a long time.

Chapter 3

Sam slept at Maire's place for two days. He had awakened the first morning to find Madsen feeding Beatrice a beef bone, then he had drifted back to sleep. Not once did he have the persistent nightmare which often awakened him in the night, soaked in sweat, still lingering in a dream world where he was struggling in vain to close the wounds on Kira's mangled face.

He awakened again later, this time to the smell of smoke and hot wax. Through his sleep-induced stupor he could see Madsen in front of an altar aglow with candles. After Sam mumbled something about a smoke detector, Madsen crawled back into bed next to him then pulled the sheet up over his chest and waited until he drifted off again.

When he finally crawled out of his half-coma the second morning, he stumbled to the kitchen to find Maire. There they drank a pot of steaming chicory coffee as the late morning sun glinted off her long, silky legs. Sam quietly listened as she filled him in on her life since they had last seen each other. He knew she would wait patiently until he felt he could do the same.

"Convince me again why it was a good idea that we never slept together," Sam teased her.

"You know you were underage when we met. Then you got pinned to that uptight sorority girl at Tulane, and that's when I became persona non grata."

"Never persona non grata to me. But maybe to uptight Simone."

"After you and Simone headed to Pepperdine Law School, I thought that was the last I'd hear from you except for the occasional scraps of information from Duval. I must admit I was pleased when you occasionally stayed in touch. So why is it you never practiced law after passing the bar, Sam?"

"I found law to be about as exciting as a Tabasco colonic. If I had given it enough time, I might have found a branch of law I liked, but joining the Marines felt right at the time. Maybe I was just trying to get away from Simone," he grinned.

"Well, that's the one thing that does make sense!"

"Before I met Kira, I did come back to see you. That's when I heard you had married and moved to Martinique. I was jealous *and* envious."

"It was nice until my reprobate husband gambled away most of our money. I left him there and came back here to the only other place I had known as home. By then, you were gone forever. At least that's what I thought. It seemed as though timing was never on our side, chere. But here you are, and for once we are both free."

"You know I'm still dealing with endings, right?"

"Yes. And I am here first and foremost as a friend."

"Thank you."

"I don't know what I want either. I know what I *don't* want is complications. Let's take it slow and see where it goes."

"That would be interesting. And very nice."

"You're the only man who has never judged me for my profession, Sam."

"I hope that's a quid pro quo. We cops aren't exactly moralistic."

"Ah, I know you were never a dirty cop. And believe it or not, I had my standards also."

"That's probably the real reason you never slept with me."

"Ha, I certainly should have! Throughout my life I've only slept with men I cared about, and never for money. I bought this business at an early age to support myself, and I never saw it as anything but business. Nevertheless, I am not exactly held in high esteem by the Junior League."

Sam smiled, "Well I am sure the Junior Cadets adore you."

* * *

After breakfast, as Sam reclined on the veranda swing, the heat closed in like a wet blanket. Celeste, flaunting all her blond hair and ripe sensuality, stepped out to greet him with a frosty margarita, which Sam gratefully accepted.

"Why don't you stick around awhile now that you've caught up on your sleep?" Celeste suggested as she leaned against the wooden door frame. "I could show you what New Orleans has to offer." When she shifted her legs under her wrap skirt, it was apparent she was wearing nothing under the clinging fabric. She spread her legs and fanned the hem of her skirt with one hand to cool her thighs while she tossed her blond hair away from her neck and licked the sweat off her lip.

"It's hot enough already, Celeste," Sam grinned appreciatively. He knew when he was being worked. "I think I'll go inside before I suffer a meltdown."

"You can't be celibate forever, handsome," Celeste said to his back as he walked away. "I know a primed pump when I see one."

Sam paused–was he that obvious? Didn't matter, he reminded himself as he shoved the door open, unless he and Maire still had something, he wasn't going to go that route. He had let Madsen comfort him like a drug fix to kill the pain, but with most people, he preferred distance.

When Sam finally entered the parlor, he spotted Madsen. She was sitting primly upright on the divan as though she had been waiting awhile. "Mr. Lerner, do you think we could talk sometime? It's kind of important."

Sam wasn't too sure how to read Madsen's agitation, but it was barely disguised by her polite demeanor as she yanked her silver pendant back and forth along its long chain. He had been known to rattle the nerves of a lot of people in his better days, but they had usually been suspects.

"Call me Sam," he said gently, "and of course, we can talk now, Madsen. I'm in no hurry to leave."

"No, Maire says I'm to let you be for now. Until you adjust, she said. So I wanted to know if maybe when you come back we can talk?" Madsen smiled tentatively then tugged her pendant again.

"Sure. I'll be back around soon to visit," he assured her before pulling out his wallet. Sam was quite surprised when Madsen refused to accept his money.

"No, Mr., um I mean, Sam. It was so nice. It's like being friends."

Sam gently reached out to still her hand as she continued to pull at her pendant. "Yes, it is, Madsen. Friends."

* * *

That had been five days earlier. Standing now in the kitchen of the old family home, he was feeling hang-dog guilty about hiding in his self-imposed seclusion. He really preferred to avoid human interaction, except on his own terms, but he couldn't get Madsen's sincere face out of his mind. He just didn't want to be anybody's friend right now–that's how he needed it. However, Sam had promised her they would talk, and he was a man of his word. Perhaps he'd drop by Maire's place later.

The battered farm house in St. Bernard Parish was just outside Chalmette. He and his father had moved there after his mother died and they left St. Tammany. He had inherited the property, and he knew there would be some sales potential in it if he cleaned it up and cleared the land. Besides, he was still too spent to go anywhere else too soon, even if he could find a direction.

Sam had substantial savings, and there was money from Kira's life insurance policy. Ironic, he often thought, how Kira's death provided money to keep him alive when he would have preferred to die with her.

Sam sighed. It was only 9:00 A.M. and the air was already thick with heat. He haphazardly began to unpack a few boxes with no clue as to how to organize things. He yanked open a kitchen drawer where he had already stashed away his S & W snub nose .38 and a can opener. How convenient, he observed wryly–if the can opener were to break, he could just blow the top off the can with his piece. That was as good a place as any for his socks, too, he figured. Why over-think it?

Just as he was unloading a few dishes, he heard a car pull up the dirt road alongside the house. Beatrice opened one eye but made no effort to move. "You're supposed to *discourage* guests, girl," Sam admonished on his way to the screen door. "I'm surprised you're not firing up the barbecue!"

He saw a huge shadow as it fell across the porch and absorbed the morning light. Sam knew who it was even before Leon Duval lumbered into his own silhouette and came to a standstill.

"'Morning, Duval," San drawled. "Am I wanted for becoming a Lakers fan, or are you just dropping by to look over our old high school year book?" Sam knew his remark landed with a bit more bite than he intended. Although Duval liked to relive the past, Sam was in no mood to explain how he was having a hard enough time just trying to hold on to the present.

"Not exactly either," Duval answered matter-of-factly. He pushed through the door with a case of beer in hand. "I'm here on business. Jesus it's hard to breathe. The air's like one big steamin' cow paddy!"

Sam followed him to the kitchen where Duval unloaded the beer on the counter. "Business, eh? You opening up a speakeasy?"

"No, I'm opening up a new case. And I need your cooperation."

"What in the hell do you need *my* cooperation for?"

Duval shifted on his large feet as he looked around the room. "Well, Sammy, I got kind of a nuisance case I've got to tie up. I got me a citizen who went missin' just over a week ago, and I'm already up to my ass in a turd stew. I'm clean outta steam. I've been workin' overtime on another case–some runaway girl who disappeared a short while back, and then there's that priest molestation scandal, too."

"Interesting. But who'd molest a priest?"

"No, the priest did the porkin'!" After a beat, he shook his head and laughed. "Oh, hell, you're just yankin' my wang, ain't ya? 'Father Fornication' we dubbed him."

"That does have a certain ring to it."

"Yeah. Anyway, these cases hang on like stink on shit," he groused as he yanked two beers out of the case.

"Duval, are you always this scatological before breakfast?"

"Well I already ate," Duval shrugged as he held out a beer.

"No thanks, I'm trying to ease off."

Duval ignored him and tossed it Sam's way. When Sam caught the can, he noticed it was icy cold. He set the beer on the counter and decided to think about how badly he really wanted a drink. Pretty badly, as far as he could tell, but he knew he had been overdoing it, and he wasn't sure how long a guy could live if his liver crapped out. He wouldn't mind dying, it's the lingering that was unappealing. Sam restrained himself as his guest opened a can and chugged thirstily.

Beatrice wandered into the kitchen at the sound of the pop top. Sam took Duval's beer out of his hand, gave Beatrice a swig, and handed it back. Duval shrugged then took another drink. "I want to come back as a dog," he grinned. "It's true dogs look like their owners. You both could use a shave."

"Neither of us expected company or I would have polished the silver. So about this missing persons case of yours–what's the scoop? Can you cut to the chase, please?"

"It's routine, probably a runaway," Duval said dismissively. "But I was staring into a plate of ham 'n eggs 'n grits when I got the idea that you might start pokin' around a bit when you heard the news."

"Why in God's name would you think that? Do you see some private dick sign hanging on my door?" Sam yanked the back door open for emphasis, pulling off the knob in the process. He grunted in disgust and then tossed the knob into the drawer with his weapon and his socks. "Rest assured, I'm out of the crime business for good."

"I hear ya. But I was afraid you might work up an interest in local matters. And you're always Mr. Nice Guy, so I thought you might find yourself being lured back into our business down here as a way of helping folks. And if you did, you could unintentionally step on my toes."

Duval shuffled his feet self-consciously as he chose his next words with care. "See, I'm vying for another promo, Sammy, so I need to be a superstar on this. And I need to keep this under my complete control. But I'd be happy to hear any input from you," he quickly added. "We all know you're the guy with the brains. I'm just the little engine that could."

"There's nothing little about you, pal. And stuff the flattery. It's me–Sam. I know your act. So if I read between the lines here, I'm to butt out, but because you think I'll be motivated to do a bit of investigation on my own out of habit, I'm also to report to you immediately if I have any ideas or information that might help you solve the case and earn that promotion you're jonesing for."

"Sounds a bit harsh when you put it like that, but that'll do. In the meantime, I got the pussy posse combing the streets, and I'm calling in a few favors. And I'll throw a few your way, of course."

"I thought you only *accepted* favors."

"True. But I promised Maire I'd help."

"Maire? What's she got to do with this?"

Duval immediately lifted a hand in warning. "Now remember, you promised me you'd stay out of it, and I'm holding you to it. The missing person was one of Maire's girls."

"Why in the hell didn't you say that up front?"

"Because I knew how you'd react."

"Well of course you did, you prick! Anything pertaining to Maire is of interest to me. What's the girl's name?" Sam demanded.

"Madsen."

"MADSEN?"

"Are you gonna repeat everything I say?" Duval complained. "Yes, Madsen Cassaise. And I understand you met her. 'Seems right after that is when she went missing. But you are not to get involved unless it's at my discretion, you understand, old friend?" There was an unmistakably menacing tone beneath the warning. "Oh, and I should probably add that based on what happened to the last hooker who went missing, the poor girl is most likely dead."

Sam mechanically reached for the beer, popped the top, and chugged it down. He couldn't shake the image of Madsen's trusting gaze, and he knew there was not enough alcohol in New Orleans to wash down the lump in his throat.

Chapter 4

Louis Santos was sweating profusely as he scaled the levee. Although it was now dark, he wanted to avoid the tourists on the nearby walkway to the river. As he scuttled along the rise of the levee, he slipped several times on the grass, which was laden with humidity. He finally came to an old barge that was docked at the foot of the levee away from the more populated river boat landing.

Louis pulled out a cigar, bit off the end, and struck a match, waving the match slowly back and forth before lighting his cigar. He then took a long pull off the Havana and waited.

As he straightened his tie and smoothed his wet shirt, he thought about how much he hated New Orleans. It was too damn hot, too French, and the light was all wrong. He missed Baton Rouge, and he had no intention of hanging around much longer. He'd be here just long enough to finish business, collect his share and split.

Louis removed a handkerchief and wiped his brow. When he noticed a flashlight illuminate one area of the barge, he approached cautiously, keeping his face turned from the light.

"You 'ere on biznez?" the voice from the barge asked in heavy Cajun dialect as Louis got closer. The voice strained to be heard, as if leaking out through the pores in the man's throat.

"It's me, you crazy old fuck," Louis snapped. "Point that light the other way!"

"I thought it was you, but I can't see much in the dark. Co'mon 'board." The disfigured barge captain struggled to time his words with each out-breath.

Louis knew that despite the old Cajun's cordiality, he was as scared as a rodent in a buzzard's claws. And Louis enjoyed that immensely. "No, I'll stay on shore," Louis growled, "I'm just here to make the delivery, Faustin."

Louis pulled an envelope from his pocket and waved it at the man. He observed how Faustin kept his distance, his feet frozen to the deck of the barge. When he saw a shudder crawl down the old duffer's body, Louis smiled with satisfaction.

"You kin pass the money to me from dere," Faustin responded as he reached for the envelope. He kept his eyes fixed on Louis in the dim light, focusing on the heavy pouches beneath his visitor's dead eyes. He had long ago memorized Louis's meaty neck and short arms with those savage, cinder block hands.

Louis purposely let Faustin get a look at his strong frame and grinned as the barge captain struggled to suppress his trembling. After a moment, Louis abruptly pulled back out of the light and took a puff off his cigar. While he waited for Faustin to count the money, he glanced toward the river boat landing and the voices that were wafting their way.

When Faustin finished counting, he suddenly came to his senses. "Din't need ta count. 'Wasn't thinkin.' Of course I trust you. No insult intended." He shoved the envelope into his pocket and clumsily lit a long brown cigarette to ease his nerves.

In the glimmer of the lighter, Louis could see the left half of the barge captain's head. Faustin's face was covered with gnarled scar tissue so tight to the bone that the side of his face looked like a death mask. A hole marked his throat like a sunken bulls eye.

"Fuckin' gargoyle," Louis mumbled. Louis believed people deserved what they got. And he figured that was why he himself had it so good, because he deserved it. He took another long puff off his Havana and then stepped a bit closer to Faustin just to get a reaction.

"Ya shur dere's no chance of dogs detectin'?" Faustin asked as he backed further away. He squeezed out the sounds, each word fraught with tension.

"No way. And no more questions. Lookin' at you makes me wanna puke. You're getting top dollar for this business arrangement, and you're not backing out now, hear me? The rest of the money will be on the delivery end. So shut your ugly face."

"But the last attempt whar aborted. You din't say nothin' about no girls dyin' on us."

"Unfortunate accident," Louis shrugged.

"Cops gonna be checkin' on dis one, too?" Faustin prodded.

"Of course they'll come sniffin' and doing a bunch of procedural bullshit. But it's all been taken care of, so shut the fuck up about it."

"Sorry. Jus' watchin' out for m'self."

"You just watch out for *me*," Louis warned menacingly. "I'm the one delivering your future. In the meantime, keep out of sight." When Louis saw another river boat coming in close to the barge, he turned around and started to scale back up the levee.

Faustin's hand automatically went to the hole in his throat. In a self-protective urge to make sure things were smooth between him and Louis, he hustled to the edge of the barge. "No need ta rush off," he barked to Louis, "I got some whiskey here on da barge."

Louis paused to look back at the old Cajun. In the moonlight, he could see the two mismatched sides of the captain's head. "No, I can't stand your face," Louis snarled. Just don't fuck anything up, or you'll lose whatever face you've got left. Do you remember how that felt, Faustin?" Louis stamped a foot toward the old captain as if he were about to come back after him.

Faustin backed away so fast he had to grab onto an oil barrel for support. He could feel the wet seep down his pant leg as he waited for Louis to disappear over the levee. Then he abruptly unzipped his fly and relieved what was left in his bladder over the side of the barge. His face twitched, and his hands shook uncontrollably as he struggled to tuck himself back into his pants.

Chapter 5

Madsen could smell the vomit in the strands of hair that lay across her face. When she tried to brush the hair away, she discovered she couldn't move her arms. Gradually she became aware of a weight that was crushing her, but she was too tired to push against it. Every effort to move made her dizzy; and the strong odor of urine and defecation around her was overpowering. She heaved again, and the remains of her stomach retreated into her throat. Finally she began to sob until the exhaustion from the effort forced her back to sleep.

Hours later Madsen awakened once more, still dizzy and confused. When she cried out into the darkness, her own voice answered back. She blinked several times in an attempt to orient herself in the room. She knew it had to be very late because she could hear no voices or music coming from the parlor or the garden. And the degree of darkness was very strange.

She longed to hear the throbbing music that drifted up into her room each night as she entertained callers at Maire's Gentlemen's Club. She always enjoyed their company, for they kept her from feeling so lonely. And Maire's establishment had become home. It was the only real home she had ever known.

As Madsen lay still, she tried to imagine the face of her mother. Their last visit was motivated by a "message" from her divination cards that her mother needed her. Madsen had located her in a Shreveport jail where her mother had been incarcerated on charges of theft and prostitution. The swelling in her chest increased as Madsen pictured her mother. "Mama," she tried to call out, but the only sound she heard was a muffled sob.

She desperately wanted a drink of water. As Madsen struggled to lift her head, her breath was labored. Her panic mounted as the thought of suffocation overcame her. She commanded her hand to reach for the lamp.

Suddenly Madsen froze. She could not feel her body below her neck. She tried again to lift her hands, but all she could feel was her muffled screams ricocheting throughout her chest like heavy hail stones.

She cried out again, her voice growing smaller against the mocking echo. "Help! Maire? Can you help me? Oh please, somebody please help me!" she pleaded to the abyss. A dull ringing in her ears increased her dizziness. Perhaps she was drunk, she thought. But she didn't drink, she disliked liquor. Had she gone back to her room after the dinner? Had she ended up somewhere else–in someone else's bed perhaps? Madsen couldn't remember where she was, or how she got there. "Maire," she called again, "please help me!"

As the relentless vacuum pushed in, she feared she had gone blind during the night. When Madsen tried to raise her head to call for help again, it was too heavy to move. *Oh, God, I can't breathe! I have to get up.* She could no longer control the panic.

She knew she must have been very bad to be punished like this. She tried to remember all the things in her life she had done that were bad. She had always believed that ladies of the night were no different than those girls who slept around for no money at all. Her mother had told her the only difference was that professionals were good businesswomen. And her mother was a professional.

When the men her mother brought home had started having their way with Madsen, she had run away. After that she had given herself to men for money, too, which is all she knew how to do. Some said that was sinful, but Madsen remembered the many men who had come to her with sad eyes and broken hearts. Of course, some had just wanted a good time. Perhaps they were the bad ones, and she was bad for servicing them. But she couldn't understand what she had done that was evil enough to deserve this torture.

Please don't leave me here, God, she silently begged. Finally Madsen willed herself to lift her head, forcing her neck to stretch so far the strain made her head shake. She hit her head on a hard and rough surface located just inches above her face. The air around her evaporated and closed in.

Madsen was suddenly seized with overwhelming horror. She realized she was locked in a box of some sort, blanketed with nothing but endless blackness. In a moment of living death, a monstrous terror overtook her senses, and she knew she had been buried alive.

Chapter 6

Sam had spent most of the past two days driving around with Beatrice and catching up with his past, while Leon Duval's case was never far from his mind. All he had been able to think of late into the night was Madsen's few pathetic possessions and her last words to him. "Like friends," she had said, as though she had no one else.

Sam didn't want to admit how much he had been drawn to Madsen because of their mutual isolation. He hoped she had just decided to move on to a new life, but he planned to drop by Maire's just to ask a few questions to satisfy himself. But first, he had to eat.

As he cruised down Decatur in Jackson Square, he sucked in the essence of earthy river water mingled with the fragrance of strong coffee from the Cafe du Monde across the street. Beatrice sat up long enough to check out the action as a Dixieland band sauntered by. Sam liked the city on summer evenings. The air was sultry enough to keep the fish jumping and the tourist population under control.

Sam pulled over and stopped in front of Tujagues, one of his favorite restaurants in the French Quarter. He had been craving Southern home cooking and spicy ribs since his fast exodus out of Los Angeles, but earlier that morning he had resolved to forgo any alcohol chasers. After polishing off a good portion of Duval's locally-brewed housewarming gift, he was sure he had also polished off his last living brain cell.

Sam took Beatrice around the back and left her with one of the waiters who had been there since Sam was a kid. "Thanks for looking after her, James," he said as he turned toward the main dining room.

As soon as the maitre d' spotted Sam, he rushed over, wrapped his arms around him, and kissed Sam on both cheeks. "So good to see you, boy," he smiled, "I've been waiting for you to drop by. You sure are looking good–hardly aged a bit."

"Still given to hyperbole, I see. It's great to see you, too, Antoine. How have you been?"

"Aw, the arthritis still gets to me, but forget all that. Sit down and eat, Sammy. Anything you want is on the house."

"That's not necessary, but thanks for the offer. Is Duval watching out for you well enough?" Sam inquired.

"Sure. He told me you wrote to him and asked him to come by my house to help out."

"That's the least I can do for one of Jem's best pals."

"He watches over the place, and gives me a hand with my car from time to time. That's real nice of you both, son. So what'll it be–the usual for you?"

"Bring it on, Antoine." Sam pulled out a chair and looked around the old place as Antoine moved about giving orders. Tujagues was one of New Orleans' oldest restaurants, established in 1856 in a Spanish armory near the river. Over the years the restaurant had remained virtually unchanged, from the ornate Parisian mirror to the old cypress bar itself. The familiarity of the place made Sam feel grounded.

While Sam was studying the other diners pouring over their six-course meals, he noticed that his server had opened a bottle of wine and was offering him a taste for his approval. "A special gift from Antoine," the waiter told him.

Sam hesitated, but the bouquet of the Corton-Charlemagne persuaded him to renege on his pledge of abstinence. "Wow – how generous! Tell Antoine it's wonderful and that I said thank you," he said as he allowed the waiter to fill his glass. Sam slowly sipped, welcoming the wine as a congenial table companion.

As he savored the wine, Sam observed a well-dressed man at a nearby table who was watching him. When Sam looked directly at the gentleman and nodded, the man looked away. Unfriendly bastard, Sam thought as he tried to place where he had seen the guy before.

Sam subconsciously catalogued the man's expensive suit with its hand stitched lapel. Canale suit, silk, size forty-four short, with alterations, Sam determined. He suspected the man had eaten there before, as he was ordering another course without referring to the menu. When the stranger noticed Sam appraising him, he pulled a brochure from his pocket and pretended to study it.

Sam turned away and dug into the Coquilles St. Jacques the waiter had set in front of him. He had been coming to Tujagues since college when he and a frat brother named Roland had suffered from huge appetites and minimal income. They could always count on a huge meal at Tujagues, because Antoine was not only Jem's old crony, but also Roland's father.

Although Sam could hardly visualize Roland after two decades, he would never forget the night his friend was killed in a foolish incident in the Quarter. While still fresh-mouth punks, Sam and Roland had gotten into a brawl after a football game. The fight came to a halt when Roland was thrown through the window of a bar on Basin Street, severing his jugular vein. Sam remembered little more than lying in the street looking up at a horse's belly while a towering cop climbed down from the saddle. In the years that followed, Sam had stayed in touch with Antoine, helping him out whenever he could.

Sam looked up as Antoine pulled out a chair. "Leon Duval tells me you're going to fix up your father's old place. Do you have enough money?"

"Duval talks too much, especially for a cop. And yes, I get a pension. I left L.A.P.D. after twenty years to the day. Thanks for asking, Antoine."

"Don't mention it. Just remember I'm here for you. I tried to write to you when your wife died, but I couldn't do it, Sam. I couldn't put the words down. I knew the pain would rip you to pieces no matter what I said. But take it from me, it does get easier."

"It can't get much worse."

"I know, Sammy. I'm glad you got yourself a dog for company."

"Is there anything Duval forgot to mention in his report?"

"Duval didn't mention a dog. I saw your pooch when Charles was playing with her back in the kitchen. I'm glad you brought her. But if the Department of Health drops by, we'll say she's an assist dog."

"She assists me more than anyone I know."

"Golden Retriever, huh?"

"The only thing she retrieves is her feeding dish."

"Yeah, she's in the back working on one of our beef bones right now," he grinned. "Have you seen Maire yet?"

"I dropped by there my first night back. Incidentally, I'm doing some un-official investigating on a girl of hers who may be missing. Could be the girl just left town. She's biracial, early twenties–named Madsen. She has real big eyes, shoulder-length curly dark hair, small mole on her left cheek. Can you ask around and keep alert? And don't tell Duval I was asking. She probably moved on, but she could be in trouble."

"I'll do that. Now eat," Antoine said before limping off after a waiter.

As Sam speared a scallop, he noticed the stranger watching him again. The guy seemed less like a tourist and more like a frequent or long-term visitor. Sam sized up what remained of a fresh trout on the man's plate before he caught the title of the pamphlet the guy was reading–a brochure from the New Orleans aquarium. The burly guy apparently liked fish, but not so much that he wouldn't consume them. The man paid his bill with cash, checked his gold Rolex, and then threw a wad of bills down for the waiter. New money, Sam figured, admonishing himself for not leaving his propensity for professional assessment in a file cabinet back in L.A.

Sam was poking at another scallop when a fork suddenly loomed over his plate. "Do you mind?" Duval asked with a grin. He stabbed a scallop without waiting for an answer.

"Duval, where in the hell did you come from?"

"The kitchen. I saw the Shelby, and Charles just stepped outside with your pup, so I was hopin' I'd find you."

"I'm eating. Can it wait?" Sam sighed when Duval pulled out a chair and sat down without invitation. "I guess I should take that as a 'no,' " he muttered.

While Sam was flagging his waiter to request a plate for Duval, the sullen stranger at the nearby table stood to leave, dropping his napkin on the floor in the process. He smoothed the creases in his pants, kicked the napkin under the table, and then pulled out a cigar. Sam noted that although the man was so precise about his clothes, he had mud on his heels.

When the stranger lit his cigar, Sam recognized the aroma of Havana Esplendido. Not a cheap smoke. It was the same brand one of his collars, a professional hit man back in L.A., had smoked. The hit man, in an odd salute to Sam's savvy in solving the case, had sent Sam his personal stash before being incarcerated for life at Terminal Island Penitentiary.

"Hey, you wanna take that stinkin' thing outside, sir?" Duval barked close to Sam's ear. "Ya can't smoke in a restaurant!" The man stared down Duval while he took his time leaving.

Sam studied the man's gait, still trying to figure out where he had seen him before. The shape of the head looked familiar. Had he seen him at Maire's, he wondered. Or at Stanley Restaurant on Saint Ann Street that morning? It was uncharacteristic of him to forget a face. He was getting rusty.

"She's dead," Duval said matter-of-factly interrupting Sam's thoughts.

Sam was completely thrown off-guard. "Who?" he asked.

"Madsen Cassaise." Duval took a swallow of Sam's wine, swished it around his mouth and swallowed. "She's dead."

Sam felt as if he were standing on sand at high tide. He heard the words fall out of Duval's mouth like anvils, clattering onto the table as they landed helter-skelter. He reached for his wine and tried to stay tuned in to what Duval was saying.

"She had gone unidentified in the morgue awhile before I got wind of it. I had a hunch, so I sent Maire down to ID her. The victim supposedly had no family. Maire didn't want the girl to be a charity burial at potter's field out at Rest Haven, so I arranged for the body be released to Maire, who was generous enough to pay for a simple casket. Apparently she drowned in the river. The water in her lungs indicated she was still alive when she went in. The coroner said she showed signs of intoxication and drug overdose. No one knows where she went in."

"Intoxication? She told me she didn't drink."

"Hell, Sam, I'm surprised she didn't tell you she was still a damn virgin."

"So Maire was sure it was Madsen?

"Well, the girl was pretty beat up by the current, but yeah. Anyway, the victim was released from the funeral home this morning and they laid her to rest out at Lafayette Cemetery out on Washington. I tried to reach you, but seein' as how ya' don't have a phone yet and you were nowhere to be found, I had to track you down. Don't know your cell number," he shrugged.

Sam shook his head. He had gone to see Mammy Jem, and he had spoken to her about Madsen. But he was in no mood to discuss it with Duval right now. He felt like hitting something. "Well it seems you've got it all under control, Duval," Sam said as he pushed his plate away.

"Not so fast. It gets complicated from here. The mother showed up this morning."

"Her mother? You just said she had no family."

"I said "supposedly." Madsen must've lied to Maire about not havin' a family, Sam. We tried our damnedest to track down any kin just to be sure, but we turned up nothing. It seems Madsen changed her name, ID's, and all after leaving home without a trace years ago. We assumed she had told the truth about being alone, and then out of nowhere I get this girl's mother crawling up my ass like a bubblin' fart."

"How'd the mother find out?"

"Coincidence, I guess. The mama came to town from outside Picayune, Mississippi to see her daughter. Only once she gets here, her girl turns up freshly buried. I wonder if Madsen knew her mama was coming."

"Only if she heard if from you on your Midnight Ride, Revere."

"Huh?"

"Skip it."

"Look, Sam, the woman tracked her daughter to Maire's place."

"Oh, so Maire's place is in Frommer's Travel Guide now?"

"Hell, I'd give her a five star," Duval grinned. "The mama, unfortunately, is threatening to make things tough for Maire and her business. I guess she thinks Maire, as Madsen's employer, was somehow responsible for not looking out for her daughter better. Maire could find herself in some trouble that even I can't keep a lid on."

"And just where do I come in?"

"Someone uninvolved needs to calm the mother down. You could talk to Madsen's mama for me. She already knows you were one of the last persons to see her daughter. In fact, if I didn't know you better, I'd even consider you a suspect."

"Seriously, Duval?"

"Yes. It don't look good, Sammy. At the very least it makes you a person of interest. But I'm willing to overlook a few things if you can help me out."

"How convenient. So I help you out and you lay off my ass as a possible suspect."

"Hell, I'm just askin' ya to tell that Oleyant woman Maire is good to her girls, and that you were a friend to her kid."

Sam winced at Duval's choice of words. He rubbed his eyes and then placed his napkin on the table. "Jesus Christ, Duval, yesterday you wanted me to stay a mile away from this, which I was content to do, and now you're talking out of the other side of your mouth." He paused then sighed in frustration. "Okay,

I'll talk the woman down from her tree – but only for Maire's sake. Where's she staying?"

"At Maire's."

"What the hell?"

Leon shrugged. "Shit, buddy, the mama is no duchess. She was a former 'hostess' like Maire, so Maire told the woman she could stay a night or two while she packs up the victim's belongings. She thought it could help smooth things over. Just common courtesy."

"Damn I've missed all this Southern hospitality."

Duval winked lasciviously, "I hear it hasn't missed you,"

"You hear too well. And you don't see enough."

"I see enough to know you went to visit Maire. And Jem, too. How is your ol' mammy?" Duval inquired.

"Great. And stay off my tail. I've outgrown the kind of Southern comfort we grew up with back in St. Tammany. I keep to myself these days."

"You got it, buddy. I'm sorry, I didn't mean to get in your space. I just was trying to make you feel welcome 'n all. And I like to look out for my friends. If you could just handle Madsen's mother, I'd be real grateful. You're a great diplomat, Sammy. Well, when you wanna be, that is. You're better than I'll ever be."

As Duval stood up to leave, Sam felt ashamed for being so curt. He watched the big man exit, knowing he should apologize. It seemed like Duval was trying to reassemble the college team. Duval had been the formidable lineman, while Sam had gotten all the glory as the hotshot quarterback. Duval had never seemed to mind as long as they won the game and he could tag along to parties with the guys. Duval had always annoyed Sam, but they had a history.

He wanted to go after Duval to smooth things over, but as the door closed, Sam remained in his seat. He decided he would talk to Duval tomorrow, and maybe work on being a bit more civil.

He lingered a moment longer before a movement on the street caught his attention. Through the window he could see the stranger from the restaurant stepping out from the shadow of the balcony that lined the adjacent building. Streaks of light marred the man's face, giving it the appearance of broken crockery.

The man hesitated before looking over his shoulder. When the silhouette of a larger figure turned the corner just ahead of him, the stranger stepped off the curb and followed in the same direction. He was following Leon Duval.

* * *

After throwing money down on the table, Sam quickly exited Tujagues on foot, leaving Beatrice behind in the safety of the kitchen. He turned east on Decatur and ran through the dark night keeping eyes and ears alert for the sounds of a scuffle. He could no longer see Duval or the stranger.

After several blocks, Sam stopped to catch his breath. His head was pounding from the wine, and he was breathing rapidly. He was suddenly alert to the rustling sounds of someone struggling nearby. "Duval?" Sam waited several seconds for a response. The street around him was dark and deserted, which set his nerves further on edge.

While turning into a small alley near the old mint to follow the sounds, he automatically reached for a weapon that was no longer there, leaving him feeling naked and vulnerable.

Sam jumped over a fence next to the alley and found himself in a small courtyard full of roses and oleander. He ducked down behind the fountain and waited. There was no indication of disturbance in the courtyard, and no signs of life.

The footsteps started up again on the other side of the wall. Sam scaled it with little effort, his upper body still strong and muscular in spite of his shortness of breath. When he paused to listen, he realized the footsteps were not Duval's.

Sam could identify people by gait, gesture, and movement from a long distance, even when he couldn't distinctly see them. And he knew the steps he had heard were those of the man in the restaurant. But how had Duval disappeared so quickly, he wondered. Was he unconscious in an alley somewhere?

The stranger was only about twenty yards ahead in the alley behind Barracks Avenue, so Sam began running again. He followed the footsteps several more blocks, all the while fighting his urge to regurgitate his rich dinner. Suddenly the footsteps made a sharp turn towards the river. Sam felt a stab of dismay as he remembered the mud on the stranger's shoes. The guy was probably a helluva lot more familiar with the deserted river area than he was. At least they were both equally handicapped by large meals, but Sam's pounding temples were an additional liability.

When the men were far enough beyond the French Quarter to be in the vicinity of the Mandeville Street Wharf, Sam ducked behind a shack and took a moment to adjust his eyes to the blackness. There was very little moonlight, and a thick fog was rolling in. As he paused for his chest to stop heaving, he listened closely until the sound of an approaching river boat drowned out the footsteps. Sam waited patiently in hopes that the boat would provide some necessary assistance.

Just as the river boat passed, Sam scanned the top of the levee. He could barely make out a shadow moving along the rise of the levee, now slightly illuminated by the lights from the passing boat. He ran full speed after the shadow.

When he reached the top of the levee and realized he was now completely out in the open, it suddenly occurred to him this could be a trap. Why someone would be after him, he wasn't sure. After all, he wasn't a cop anymore, and he didn't reek of enough money to entice a mugger. But an assault on him might possibly be a warning intended for his cop friend, Leon Duval.

Although Sam could smell his own sweat, he shuddered in spite of the wet heat. Suddenly he yelled at the passing river boat; if he was going down, he wanted someone to witness it. Unfortunately, the grinding of the boat's engines drowned out his voice. He stayed low to the ground, listening. As the boat passed, he heard nothing but its fog horn melding into the night air. At that point Sam decided to leave the heroics to the New Orleans boys in blue.

He dropped back on the side of the levee opposite the river and slid back down the embankment until he was stopped short by what felt like a low wall of wood. When he ran his hands along the wall, he realized that what he had thought was some sort of barrier was actually a wooden packing box about six feet in length and three feet wide. Along the side of the box were a number of holes the size of his fingertips.

Crawling around the crate, he noted that there was something peculiar about the cheap, casket-like box sitting out in the open. He smelled gardenia. The scent was weak but detectable. His mind raced to locate some strong association in his mental file. He was forming a mental picture just as the fragrance became mingled with stale scent of a Havana cigar.

He heard a cracking sound. His brain registered the sound of the blow an instant before he felt it. His body became a ball of dough. When Sam reached up to feel his head, it was damp and sticky. He smelled something sweet as his face fell forward into the grass next to the crate. The footsteps grew fainter, and a low moan registered in his brain just before he blacked out.

Chapter 7

Adrift in a state somewhere between unconsciousness and lucidity, Sam focused on Jemima, who was languishing in an old rocker, her yellow-flecked eyes trying to capture his wandering gaze. In his dream-state, he had entered her home, a brightly blue painted cottage with red shutters and gingerbread trim. Its front door was one step up from the street and next to a noisy gay bar at Dauphine and Dumaine.

The words *Honne* and *Respe* were hand-painted over a crucifix mounted near the door. Sam remembered the words from his youth–"honor" and "respect," the traditional greeting on entering a Haitian home.

The notes of a Blues rift pushed back against the ever-present humidity when Sam drifted into the parlor. An altar in the corner was crowded with voodoo paraphernalia and burning candles. "Is this area still a safe place for Jem?" he asked Jem's cousin Duffault, who was cooling her with a silk fan.

Duffault laughed. "It's all gay. The most they'll do to ya around here is tie you down and style your hair!"

Sam's laugh brought him to the edge of consciousness, but then he slipped back down. He and Jem were suddenly laughing and drinking. Sam was sitting on the floor next to her while a jasmine-scented breeze tip-toed in through the narrow windows that stretched from ceiling to floor.

In his dream, Sam smiled broadly as Jem spoke, occasionally lapsing into Spanish or French. He felt shame that he had waited so long to visit, but his delay had been motivated by the fear of seeing for himself how much she had aged.

He studied her hand as she reached down to pet Beatrice. The knotted fingers were partially paralyzed, a result of her first stroke. She was now blind in one eye, and a second stroke had left her unable to get around without a pronounced limp. Sam was shocked at how old she looked compared to his last visit, but she was still sassy as hell. It scared him to think of losing her. He made another effort to crawl out of his dream, but once again he gave in to it.

"I need your help, Jemima," Sam told her. "I have a friend, a girl named Madsen, who may be in trouble. She is a follower like you."

Sam recalled stories of how Jem had been a young "mambo" in Port au Prince, a voodoo priestess of great honor. In St. Tammany, she had become legendary, as much for her hand crafted voodoo charms as for her hell-raising. Sam smiled at his memories of lazy evenings spent sitting with Jem under moss-draped cypresses on the nearby bayou analyzing life as seen through the bottom of a rum bottle.

"Can you tell me what kind of trouble Madsen is in, Jem?"

Jem nodded toward a closet with louvered doors where tucked away was an altar covered with medicine packets, cigarettes, crucifixes, rattles, and a bottle of Barbancourt. On a separate table near the altar, Jem's divination cards were laid out. The foreign objects on the altar seemed mysterious and threatening. Sensing his discomfort, she shot him a lop-sided grin, revealing a gap where her front teeth had been. "Haitian and African traditions provide protection. That's how I keep you safe, boy."

Sam indicated a painting of a deity wearing a top hat and glasses with one dark lens. "That same image was above Madsen's altar at Maire's place."

"Gede. So she was Petwo, from same Haitian spirits as me—once slaves."

"Those small ceremonial pots were on her altar, too." He indicated a govi jar which Jem had once told him held the spirit of his dead mother. As a child, he had tried to lure his mother out of the jar with her favorite dessert, bread pudding, but she hadn't come.

Sam suddenly wanted to escape the dream again, but the spicy aroma of gumbo simmering on the stove lured him back. A saxophone in the street and a fountain splashing water caressed his ears with sonorous notes.

The sound of water grew louder, and Jem slowly faded. Her voice drifted to a distant place as the decorative jar that held his mother's spirit changed shape.

In his dream, Sam was now looking at a woman's back. She was dressed in a soft yellow robe, sitting at an altar. He was lying in bed, barely awake, listening as she spoke to Beatrice. "Madsen," he called to her. His head hurt, and his neck was contorted. He tried to sit up, but he fell backwards.

"Easy fella," Madsen cautioned in a distorted voice. The voice came closer, now masculine and rough, reaching out to him from a tunnel. When he opened his eyes, Madsen disappeared, and his dream receded into a swirl of lights. Sam was on his back on the ground, looking up at a dawn sky.

* * *

"Easy now, fella. Do you want to go to a hospital?" Sam tried to focus on the dark-skinned man who was kneeling over him. A ship's horn and the smell of damp grass were signs he was somewhere near the river.

"What happened to you?" the voice asked as it slowly came together with the face. The levee, now illuminated in shades of gold, jolted Sam back into an awareness of place and time.

"I'm not sure," Sam moaned, "I guess I was mugged." He reached for the back of his head, which ached each time he moved. Then he remembered the stranger he had pursued after leaving the restaurant. His eyes scanned the levee for signs of his attacker, but they were alone. When he reached into his pocket, he was surprised to discover that his wallet and keys were still there. "Did you see anyone else around here?" Sam asked.

"No, sir. I was on my way to the dock when I thought I saw a body lying up here. I was afraid you were dead until I heard you mumbling. Do you have any idea how long you've been here?"

Sam squinted at the dawn light. "Since last night some time, I think. Can you give me a hand getting up?" When the young man helped him stand, Sam winced at the pain in his head and fought to keep his balance.

"You sure you're okay? That's a nasty cut on the back of your head. It's pretty much coagulated now, but I'd have it looked at if I were you."

"I will, son, thanks." Sam suddenly remembered that Beatrice was still in the kitchen at Tujagues, and he knew he had to get to her. He took a few steps, but he stumbled several times before regaining his balance. The kid continued to watch him, obviously concerned about his wellbeing.

Sam looked down at the ground to keep from stumbling again. Something odd made him pause in his tracks. He could make out a distinct depression in the dew covered grass. The indentation was the size and shape of a coffin. There were marks in the grass where the box had been dragged down the other side of the embankment to the water's edge. But there was no loading dock there. What had he stumbled upon?

Sam shook off his confusion as he slowly pieced together the events leading up to his attack. He had finally gone to see Jem earlier in the day, and after leaving her, he had gone to Tujagues for supper. *Ah, yes, he had followed the stranger from the restaurant.* He was attacked and then lost consciousness. His dream of Jem had actually been a recollection of their visit earlier that day.

As Sam tried to recall more details, he looked around the area, visually scanning every tree within proximity. He was certain he had smelled gardenia the night before when crouching near the wood crate. But there wasn't a gardenia bush anywhere in sight. The scent had disappeared along with the coffin-like box.

* * *

By the time Sam got back to the restaurant the sun had heated the morning mist, leaving a steam in the air that was already settling in on the day. The cleaning crew opened the door of Tujagues for him, allowing him to retrieve a very excited Beatrice. After he fed her, he took her out and told her to relieve herself wherever she damn well pleased. She chose a planter that needed watering. He filled her bowl with a sprinkling can from a nearby stoop, and waited while she drank.

"Sam, what in the hell happened to you?" a voice suddenly boomed from behind. The sound resonated through Sam's skull like buckshot. Sam turned to face Leon Duval.

"Christ, Duval. I was afraid you were dead. Now I almost wish you were. Can you please keep it down?"

"You been on a binge?"

"Hell, no! I-"

Duval cut him off. "Look at the back of your head! What the fuck?" Before Sam could anticipate Duval's next move, Duval scooped up Beatrice's water dish and threw the water at the back of Sam's head. With one meaty hand, he pulled Sam close to examine the wound.

"What the fuck! Easy, Duval!" Sam yelled.

"Let me have a look at that." He welded his hands to Sam's shoulders so tightly Sam could not pull away. "It's okay, the wound is closed. Sorry about the water."

"Yeah, well you should be, asshole. At least I'm conscious now. What are you doing up so early?" He raised a brow at Duval's disheveled clothes.

"Never went home. I watched TV at Charlie Biscay's then spent the night on his couch. Big mistake. More uncomfortable than a Mormon pew. Incidentally, Charlie still owns that floral shop over in the Garden District and he wants you to drop by."

"I plan to."

"He's been waiting to see you. I told him you were back in town"

"Of course you did. Now please stop talking. I feel like I'm wearing a meat cleaver for a hat."

Duval looked contrite. "Well you asked why I was here. Charlie now lives upstairs in the building next to Tujagues."

"I know. So is that where you disappeared last night?"

"Huh?"

"I could confirm this with Charlie?"

"What are you drilling me for?"

"Forget it."

"Well, then tell me what happened, Sammy. I saw your car hadn't been moved, so I figured you were still partying. I knew the pooch was safe so I stayed out of your business like you asked. So what went down–bar fight? Some punk heard you was a cop and decided to feed you a shit sandwich?"

"Duval, please, no defecation talk this morning! It's only seven-fucking-A.M. My head can't handle it. I was mugged, that's all. I'm fine, and I'm leaving. Beatrice, get in the car, girl."

"You need me to write up a report?"

"No."

"How 'bout I take you to see Doc Fillet. Isn't that a hoot–a surgeon named Dr. Fillet?"

"Yeah. Hilarious."

"Only he pronounces it 'Fillet' like 'spill it.' Better for business. How 'bout I run you and the mutt over there?"

"No, but thanks. I want to get cleaned up. I'll drop by Maire's later to talk to Madsen's mother for you like you asked, although I can't see the point."

"Thanks, Sam, but don't waste too much time. Madsen was just another mixed up escort girl."

"She's somebody's kid, Duval."

"*Was*, Sam. But if you find out anything, you let me know."

Sam nodded then turned away. "That's not the way I work, buddy," Sam mumbled as he crawled into the Shelby. Right now he had other business to tend to. This had become a personal matter. Someone was after him. It was a warning, or he'd be dead. Something was stinking in the city, and it sure as hell wasn't just the river.

Chapter 8

While Sam showered, he wondered if Dr. Fillet could live up to his name and fillet his skull to remove the ringing from his ears. The blow to his head had also left him with waves of nausea. After he dressed he tried to eat some plain toast, then he drank three cups of strong coffee.

As he glanced over the paper, he made mental notes of what was happening locally, including the disappearance of another girl around Madsen's age. The missing girl, identified as Carol Stone, also had no kin. Her landlady reported her missing, but friends said she never stayed in one city too long. Must be the case Duval had referred to, Sam thought. He automatically filed it away.

When he felt more alert, he brought in a few boxes from the trunk of his car and a card table he had picked up to use as a desk. After he peeled the tape off a box and lifted out his computer and his papers, he spotted a photo of Kira on top of the heap. Her auburn hair was pulled back into a long ponytail, and she was smiling as though she would go on breathing forever. She was sitting on the edge of a boat off the coast of Cozumel where they had spent their last vacation. The photo had been tucked into a birthday card she had given him. He flipped it over to read the inscription he had long ago memorized: "I love you, Sweetheart."

"I love you too, babe," Sam said aloud before he tucked the photo under his keyboard. He couldn't leave it out where he'd have to look at it every day. He needed distance. Somehow he knew she would understand.

Resting his head in his hands, he fought the urge to reach for the bottle of bourbon taunting him from the window sill. Sam really wanted to forget everything that had transpired since his arrival back in the Big Easy. He had inadvertently become involved in something he could not yet define, and he had a nasty gash on his head to show for it.

Resorting to his old habit of mental flogging, Sam reviewed the mistakes he had made during the pursuit of his unknown nemesis: no light, no weapon, only a vague knowledge of the landscape. He should have called for help or had someone try to establish radio contact with Duval to make sure Duval was safe.

When starting the pursuit, Sam had never even considered that he might be outnumbered. He knew he was slightly out of shape, and maybe half out of his mind. The booze had clogged his brain. Except for his years at Tulane, he had never been much of a drinker until Kira died. Then he deliberately chose booze to medicate his pain. For a long time, Sam had suspected he was killing himself, but he hadn't had any reason to stop. But now he at least had a reason to delay it. When Sam touched his head wound, he realized just how pissed he was. If he was going to die, he decided, it would be by his own hand, not someone else's.

Sam stood up and searched through his box of belongings. He knew what he wanted was in the box somewhere. His instinct for self-survival had motivated him to dig up some information before leaving Los Angeles. When he found the paper he was looking for, he stared at the number scrawled across the page in black ink like a bitter accusation.

While he dialed the number, he pushed aside his keyboard and glanced again at the photo of his late wife. After a pause, Sam finally spoke. "Is this A.A.?" he asked hoarsely as Kira smiled up at him.

Chapter 9

"So you know my girl, Mr. Lerner?" the dark woman asked Sam. She was wearing a turquoise kerchief around her head, a yellow cotton blouse and a red skirt. Sam rubbed his aching skull and averted his eyes. She was far too vivid for Sam to focus on this morning.

"I've met her," he told Madsen's mother. "She was lovely."

"Really? Is she?"

Sam sorted through the possessions in Madsen's room as he pondered the woman's odd response and use of the present tense when referring to her daughter.

"You, uh, didn't have much contact?" he asked, noticing that the woman had beautiful eyes like her daughter.

"She's been gone since she was twelve. I'm a working woman. I didn't have time to chase her down."

Sam observed the woman's graceful movements. She had long, slender fingers adorned with gold rings. Her hands mesmerized him. They were perhaps the most beautiful hands he had ever seen. Her hands stroked the air like flowing water when she spoke. He memorized her hands for his mental fact file: Size 6 1\2 glove, he was sure. Size six ring.

"Why did Madsen leave Picayune, do you know?"

"She hated my means of providin.' Seems a few of my clients found their way with her. Did you?"

It was interesting to him how she fired her words from point blank range. "No, I did not," Sam stated, holding her gaze.

"I came for her because she needed me."

"Did she contact you?"

"In our way. The local priestess told me to come."

"Ah, yes," Sam nodded.

"I can tell you're skeptical," she interrupted. "I can also tell you have a terrible headache."

Sam grunted, unimpressed. A person wouldn't need much vision to spot a reprobate in a head bandage. His eyeballs were practically hemorrhaging. "Mrs. Cassaise-"

"No, it's 'Oleyant,' " she corrected him. "Madsen changed her name. Ashamed I guess, but then she ended up followin' in my footsteps after all. But it's not a bad livin' if you don't have a man of your own to provide for you."

"I suppose you're right. Mrs. Oleyant. Would you have any way of knowing about her friends?"

"She doesn't have friends."

Sam smarted at her words. Madsen had thought his asking nothing more of her than a shared bed to sleep in constituted being friends. Perhaps Madsen was right–wasn't a friend what he really needed, too? She had sensed that and had stayed by his side for three days. Now Sam felt uncommonly sad at the thought of her life ending in a cold, dark river.

Sam touched the woman's hand, surprised at how warm it seemed. Her skin felt creamy, almost moist. "I can't express how sorry I am that she died, Mrs. Oleyant," Sam said quietly.

It was true, he couldn't. No more than he was able to express his grief over Kira being killed. It had happened as he watched, and he had watched it over and over again in the agonizing nightmares he had suffered so many times since that night.

Madsen's mother interrupted his thoughts. "She's alive. She's not dead, Mr. Lerner."

Sam closed his eyes. He knew this song of denial well. It was his favorite top-ten hit: "It Ain't So." *Gotta great beat, easy to dance to,* he said to himself. People like him who knew the song by heart wanted to believe that if you denied death enough you could erase it. Wrong.

"Mrs. Oleyant," he said gently, "Madsen has been buried. I'll be glad to take you out to the cemetery to her grave site."

"I been there. She's not dead. But she's in trouble. Mothers know these things," she explained.

Sam tried to hide his frustration as he stared at the crude painting of a voodoo deity mounted over Madsen's altar. The deity grinned at him like a carnival barker in his top hat and glasses. Sam wondered what drug the smiling fool was on. And where he could get it.

While weighing how to handle Madsen's mother, Sam continued to walk around the room. Nothing seemed different beyond a few pieces of fruit turning brown. He opened the closet door and touched the soft chenille robe that was still hanging on its hook. Then he walked to the bureau and opened each drawer. He looked through Madsen's few possessions with as much respect as possible, memorizing each detail while her mother looked on.

There was a collection of travel brochures from cities around New Orleans and from landmarks like the aquarium, several plantation homes, and even an alligator farm. A book about movie stars and Alcott's *Little Women* were hidden beneath clean cotton panties. A used bus ticket from Baton Rouge, and a seat stub for a seat on a bus from Belle Amie, no date, were on the bottom of the pile. The bus ticket from Baton Rouge to New Orleans was dated for three months earlier. Sam smiled at the small framed picture of actor Bradley Cooper, which Madsen had evidently clipped from a magazine.

"You seem to know where things are," the woman observed.

"Just checking for indications of flight," he said in his most professional tone. "No one seems to know where she was before she drowned."

He closed the drawer and turned around just as Celeste stepped into the room. Her blond hair looked very unkempt, and her ample cleavage threatened to rupture forth from her loose kimono with every breath she took. Sam could feel his ears flush. He marveled at how Celeste had a way of making the air feel raw.

"I heard you were here," Celeste said seductively. "Please drop by my room at the end of the hall before you leave." She gave Mrs. Oleyant a tight smile before departing.

Madsen's mother was studying Sam with a look he was sure could strip paint off a wall. Her comment was unexpected. "You have Cajun spice in you. How much is Cajun?"

"One quarter."

"You are handsome. And honest. You can help me." Mrs. Oleyant reached into her handbag and offered him a photo. It was of Madsen, smiling sweetly, sitting on the front porch swing of the Gentlemen's Club. "Keep this for now. I want you to find out the details surrounding my daughter's disappearance."

Sam hesitated. He did not want to commit to staying around long enough to help out. Besides, this was no business of his. Reluctantly he shoved the photo into his wallet while Madsen's mother continued to stare at him curiously. The feeling that she was looking through him made him uncomfortable, and Sam wanted to end their visit. As he walked toward the bed, Sam made it a point to brush up against the chime mounted near the headboard.

Instantly Maire was standing in the doorway. "Can you help me lift something, chere?" she asked in her mellifluous voice. It was their routine. She was giving him an out worthy of a Southern politician. When Mrs. Oleyant nodded her dismissal, Sam smiled and completed his escape without losing a vote.

"Thanks for bailing me out, Maire," he said as he followed her to the parlor. "By the way, do you know if Madsen ever stayed somewhere else? She kept very few possessions here."

"I can't say, chere, but I doubt it. She was just poor, and very much alone. But who's to say?"

"How long did she work for you?"

"Maybe two, three months."

"Do you know where Madsen most recently came in from? She obviously left Picayune a long time ago."

"A bus ticket from Baton Rouge was in her drawer," Maire offered. "Might still be there. Feel free to look."

"I saw it. The date would fit. How did you know it was there, Maire?" Sam teased as one brow shot up. In truth he was never surprised by her vast sources of information.

"It's my place to know these things, Sam Lerner. I run a first-class guest house."

"Indeed, you do, darlin.' I'm just digging around because Duval told me she'd been dead awhile when he sent you over to identify the body. According to him, she'd been missing longer than that, which implies she was gone a few days before she drowned."

"Yes, I believe she left the same day you did. She was probably planning to just drift off. Most do sooner or later. Except the older ones. I take them out back and shoot them," she grinned.

"Oh, yeah, you're such a hardass," he smiled as he stepped onto the veranda. "By the way, did Madsen have any regular callers?"

"No one special."

"Well, if you remember anything, just call. I have a phone now. And let me know if anyone requests her specifically."

"Of course. How long do you plan to stay in New Orleans, chere?"

"I don't make plans anymore."

"Then come by. I've been thinking–maybe we should consider that 'date' we've put off all these years."

Sam stopped in his tracks. "My old love deigns herself available?" Sam shook his head slowly from side to side in wonder.

"Perhaps," she said coyly.

"But you don't sleep with-"

"Customers? You've never been a customer. You're my Sam."

"My timing in life truly sucks, Maire my love. You know I can't go there just yet. I'm not over, well, you know-"

"I know. That's why I offered," she smiled, and then she slowly closed the screen door.

Chapter 10

Charlie Biscay leaned over the old wrought iron balcony trying to catch a breeze off Decatur Street. Periodically he poured water from a can onto one of the scores of flowering plants he had arranged in vivid groups of color along the balcony. A small fountain in one corner was made of marble and featured two young boys urinating.

To Sam, Charlie's balcony looked like a parade float. His nose felt like a catcher's mitt from the overload of pollen, and he could feel another headache coming on. When Sam sneezed loudly, Charlie let out a squeal of surprise before turning his attention back to his plants.

Sam had been off booze for several days, but his head had been throbbing the entire time. When he had finally seen a doctor, he learned he had sustained a concussion from his head wound. Sam concluded he had been hit by a board of some sort, because he had been picking splinters out of his head and neck since the attack.

As Sam sat on Charlie's balcony, he watched two large women who were apparently heading for Tujagues Restaurant, which was just below and slightly west of Charlie's flat. Suddenly one woman yelled up at Charlie as the water run-off anointed her over-coiffed pink hair.

"Diseased troll," Charlie muttered under his breath. He then let out a sigh, flashed a practiced smile, and waved apologetically before lowering himself into a wicker rocker.

After he adjusted a silk scarf around his neck, he picked up his old cat and took a long drag off a joint. Charlie offered the bud to the cat and smiled when the cat loudly reprimanded him. "You're so bitchy, Barbra," Charlie laughed. He stroked the cat's patchy fur before turning his attention to Sam.

"You look very well, Sam. Age has made that face of yours even more interesting. I wish I could say the same for my own." He offered the joint to Sam, who declined.

"I know you haven't been well, Charlie. And I was real sorry to hear Dexter died."

"Thanks. I really loved that man. Twenty-three years is a good relationship, especially for us queens. This disease has no mercy. It's been pretty rough, Sam."

"I know, buddy. Duval told me you're full-blown."

"Better to be blown than blue," Charlie joked half-heartedly. "I got treatment too late. Denial is a killer." As Charlie poured more iced coffee, his thin arms were unsteady. The raised brownish-red scales of Kaposi Sarcoma were visible beneath the heavy make-up he had applied to his hands and face.

"These spots look like leeches, don't they?" Charlie asked without looking up. "They're growing like teenagers–I'm thinking about getting them drivers' permits."

"How are you fixed for emergency care, Charlie?"

"Well, there's money from my floral business, and I'm going back to the family plantation when it comes time to prepare for my eternal resting place, which I hope is a gay bath house where all the saints have great fashion sense and nice round asses."

"Nice visual. Your family home is on Bayou Lafourche, isn't it?"

"Good memory, Sambo. Do come see me off, will you? I'll dress up like Bette Davis did in *Hush, Hush Sweet Charlotte*. I'll be a sight to behold. Make them plant me with my boa on, and not too much blush. And what do you think about my little sequined number for the send-off?"

"I'm usually not the person one consults for fashion details," Sam said as he shifted in his chair.

Sensing Sam's discomfort, Charlie gently placed a hand on his shoulder. "I'm okay with it," he smiled sadly. "Bette said it best: 'Old age ain't for sissies.' And I am such a sissy. It's best I make my farewells while I'm still gorgeous."

"I'm sorry I haven't been around much in recent years, Charlie. I probably could have lent you a hand with the business and all."

"No need. Leon Duval helps me out some. He's a bit of a blockhead sometimes, but he's good. He's not the homophobe he was when we were at Tulane. I guess we all grow up. He picks up medicine for me and watches a movie with me every now and then. And he loves that I'll bet on sports with him even though I don't know football from foot odor. He hasn't figured out that I don't mind losing to him in exchange for the company. Besides, I never pay up."

"Did he come up here the night I got my brains rearranged?" Sam inquired.

"Yes, he mentioned seeing you earlier at Tujagues. He likes to sleep on my couch sometimes. Since Linny Lard-ass left him, he gets a little lonely. And I admit, it still impresses my nancy friends when a man in uniform stumbles out of my flat in the wee hours, even one with no fashion sense. Who on earth cuts that man's hair anyway?"

Sam laughed. He had always enjoyed Charlie's friendship, in spite of Charlie's penchant for push-up bras. But Sam today had more on his mind than a casual visit. He waited for his friend to take another toke before getting down to business.

"Charlie, did you ever meet an escort named Madsen? I know Maire's girls took their clientele to the same bistros you often frequent."

Charlie sat quietly for a moment before getting up to pull some dead leaves off a geranium. Sam studied Charlie's body language as his host nervously tugged at the leaves. "I'm not sure I recall anyone of that name," Charlie answered quietly.

Sam suddenly noticed something nestled among the stems of the plant Charlie was pruning. He got up and walked over to the plant. Reaching between the leaves, he pulled out a small stuffed canary.

"Where did you get this?" Sam asked.

"Cute, huh? I put them on a lot of the plants we deliver. Rubbers for the faggots and birds for the straights. It's kind of a trademark. It's a bitch when the plants get switched. Lots of folks collect them, the canaries that is."

"Madsen had a lot of these birds in her room."

"Maybe she got flowers from my store as gifts, although we don't deliver much to Maire's-" Charlie stopped mid-sentence as he glanced down toward the street. "Well lookee here, Sammy—it seems we got company."

Sam leaned over the balcony just as Leon Duval stepped into view. He looked at Duval and then glanced back long enough to see Charlie duck back inside.

"I thought I'd find you here," Duval called up to him.

"You're after me like a bad conscience. What made you think I'd be here?"

"I'm a brilliant cop. That and the fact that your car is parked around the corner and you weren't in Tujagues. I gotta talk to you, buddy."

"Whatever it is, please leave me out of it. My skull has been customized and I'm in a piss-poor mood."

"But I need your advice. Please."

"Ah, shit," Sam muttered, "I hate it when people use that word. What do you 'need' now, Duval?"

"Well, I'm in a bit of a mess. Madsen's mother is demanding a disinterment."

"What-?"

"You know, open the grave."

"I know what it *means*. But why?"

"Some spooky voodoo crappola. She can't accept the fact that the girl is dead."

"What did you tell her?"

"I told her we could do it right after I dig up Amelia Earhart."

Sam sighed with exasperation. "Still the smooth talker you always were. Don't move. I'm coming down."

* * *

When Sam stepped off the stoop onto the pavement, the heat burned through the soles of his shoes. The increased air pressure suggested evening rain. Duval was leaning his ample frame against his car as Sam approached. He rubbed the sweat off his face with the back of his hand then reached into his car to pull out a six-pack.

When Duval held out a brew, Sam shook his head and unconsciously stepped back a few feet. "No thanks, Duval. I'm off the stuff."

"Oh, fuck that. You've been through hell, and you deserve a little something to relax your nerves. This hardly has any alcohol in it. Besides, it's hotter than a turd on a grill out here." He pulled the tab off a can and pressed it into Sam's hand.

Sam could smell the beer as he shoved it away. "No thanks. I really quit."

"Cold turkey?"

"Cold turkey. With the help of a keg of Advil and a twelve-step program."

"Sammy, now what'd you go and do that for? Those programs are like new-age religions. That's L.A. kind of thinking. It just ain't normal. And it don't feel right with you standing there like some parson with a pole up his pucker."

"You'll get used to it," Sam laughed. "Probably before I will. Besides, aren't you on duty?"

"Nope, it's my day off. I ran into Madsen's mama over at Maire's. She has a helluva nerve demanding that we open the grave. She hasn't been in the girl's life for years. And we took good care of Madsen. That Oleyant woman is now using some burial ritual practiced in their ersatz religion as a legal excuse to claim the body."

"Well, she probably feels like she didn't really have a chance to say good-bye to Madsen without seeing her." He knew the feeling all too well. His wife's memorial had been a closed casket affair because her injuries were so bad. To this day, he couldn't imagine how all the life that was once Kira was stuffed into a sealed mahogany box. And he never felt he had really said good-bye.

"Sam, Maire did real nice by that girl. It cost her a fair bit to bury her and have a headstone made. I even got some public funds thrown her way for the crypt to make it a little easier on Maire. After all, she was just Maire's employee. Now this woman blows into town and wants to haul the body out of the grave, and for what?"

"Maybe you need to be a bit more sympathetic."

"Oh hell, Sam. I hope you're not advising me to go along with this! That woman was practically a stranger to the victim. And it will take weeks and a shitload of paperwork on the off chance that we can get a court order. Besides, the mother doesn't have the money to transport the dead girl back to Picayune and re-plant her, so we'll get stuck with that, too. I'm gonna get my ass stuck in a wringer for helping out in the first place. It's just not practical."

"Duval, you asked my advice. I say you go along with it. Something about Ms. Oleyant tells me she won't let the matter rest until she has her daughter back. Perhaps she's been trying to somehow get her back since the girl left. This may be her last chance."

Duval sighed and tossed his empty beer can at the trash receptacle. He missed. "Hey, kid, can you get that for me?" he called to a young boy walking by. The boy dutifully picked up the can, tossed it in the barrel, then shot the bird to Duval as he sauntered off. Duval shot the bird back at him.

"Okay," he continued, "I'll start the paperwork, but it will take time. I heard Ms. Oleyant really took to you, so can you use your good looks to charm the lady off my back for a while? I don't have time for her melodrama."

"I don't have time for yours, Duval."

"Can't you help me just a little? I've been lookin' out for your Mammy Jem pretty good for you all these years, you know. I get my men to check in on the ol' gal and to control the riffraff in the bar next door so she don't have to concern herself."

"Yeah, and I paid you to do it. Look, I'll talk with Ms. Oleyant if I see her. But let me ask you something—why did you order me not to get involved, and yet you keep trying to drag me into all this?"

Duval grinned as he climbed into his car. "If you really want to know, I was hoping a sniff of the old detective work might make you crave a shield again. I sure could use someone here with your brains and record of solves to be backing me up, just like I covered your ass at Tulane. You know you could have gone pro until you blew out that knee, but I never failed to have your back."

"And you never failed to mention it."

Duval laughed as he pulled away from the curb. "Well, we do make a great team. Think about it, Sammy," he yelled.

Sam was suddenly too preoccupied to think about Duval's offer. A dark-haired man was watching them closely from a Lincoln parked near the corner of Dumaine and Decatur. It occurred to him that he had first noticed the car when he was sitting on Charlie's balcony.

As he walked toward the Shelby, Sam subtly kept an eye on the stranger. The shadow from the car's visor fell across the man's face distorting his image.

When Sam got into his car and pulled away from the curb, the Lincoln pulled out behind him.

* * *

While taking a circuitous route to Maire's Gentlemen's Club, Sam kept a close eye on the Lincoln. The car stayed far enough away that the driver's face remained obscured. Sam slowed to turn the corner on Bourbon Street before moving slowly up Ursulines where the light was brighter. In his rear view mirror he saw the Lincoln turn to follow.

When a trash pick-up vehicle pulled out in front of the Lincoln, Sam saw his opportunity and gunned it, smiling as the Shelby responded with gusto. Sam wheeled into an alley and made a rapid U-turn between the old brick buildings. He straightened the wheel and pointed the Shelby back onto Ursulines, pulling out directly behind the Lincoln.

The driver of the Lincoln heard the squeal of tires on pavement, and checked his mirror. When he spotted Sam on his tail, he stepped on the gas and turned onto North Rampart before continuing up St. Philip, weaving around Louis Armstrong Park.

Sam knew the Shelby could easily outrun the Lincoln, but traffic prevented him from pulling alongside. He memorized the license plate, which indicated the car was purchased from a dealer in Ponchatoula, but Ponchatoula was misspelled. It would be a waste of time to run what was obviously a bogus plate.

The Lincoln seemed to be heading for the interstate until the car abruptly cut left. Sam stomped on the brakes as the Lincoln swerved onto North Villere. The sweat burned Sam's eyes as he fought to keep the Shelby under control. Spotting a break in the oncoming traffic, he turned out into the opposite lane and accelerated until he pulled up even with the Lincoln's back bumper.

Suddenly a cop on a motorcycle peeled out at the corner of North Villere and Lafitte. The officer flashed his lights as he rolled into the intersection. Following close behind the motorcycle was a funeral procession comprised of what Sam estimated to be about fifty mourners on foot. As they spilled into the intersection they were playing horns and swinging noisemakers in a send-off celebration for the departed loved one, whom they were apparently carrying to nearby St. Louis Cemetery.

All at once the music stopped as one hundred startled eyes fixed on the Lincoln and the Shelby, which were bearing down on the procession. Terrified mourners suddenly ran in every direction. The cop braked hard, forcing the motorcycle to slide on its side as he tried in vain to stop its forward momentum.

Sam made a hard left to avoid the cop. The Shelby jumped the curb before he could bring the car to a halt. He turned back to see his pursuer in the Lincoln dodging mourners as he squealed along the blacktop.

When the Lincoln turned in the direction of the interstate, the crowd closed back in around the fallen motorcycle officer, who was glaring at Sam.

Sam's turned his eyes back in the direction in which the Lincoln had disappeared. He had gotten a glimpse of his pursuer's profile, his head tilt, and the proximity of head to shoulders. The man's body movements indicated right hand dominance. The fit of the jacket the man was wearing suggested expensive taste and good tailoring to fit strong, compact shoulders.

Sam was sure his pursuer was the stranger from Tujagues Restaurant, the same sonuvabitch who must have attacked him. He had a vague memory of also seeing the guy in the shadows of the courtyard at Maire's place. What he couldn't figure out was why he was the man's object of sadistic affection. But he was sure it had something to do with Madsen Cassaise.

Chapter 11

When Sam arrived at Maire's place, it was quiet, as it usually was on an afternoon. The carefully cultivated gentility of the establishment always made him feel as if he were calling for a prom date. Well, maybe a professional prom date.

Odd, he thought, how he had lost his once avid interest in sensual pleasures and now desired little more than a brandy and a quiet conversation with Maire.

When Sam opened the door to enter the Gentlemen's Club, Celeste suddenly appeared, all bounce and hot breath. She reminded Sam of a female Fagin, waiting to lead Oliver Twist down the path of sin. Sam couldn't help but notice the shapely legs that kept peeking through the slits in the silky skirt that massaged her body with every step she took. The path of sin could certainly be an attractive little romp, Sam decided. For someone else.

"Celeste, just the person I wanted to see," Sam said by way of greeting.

"That's what every girl wants to hear, honey. I'm all yours."

"Good. Can we skip the formalities and go on up to your room?"

"Jesus, pussycat, you go from one to sixty faster than that car of yours. Come with me."

Sam followed Celeste's undulating hips past Madsen's room. They turned the corner into the east wing where Celeste occupied the corner room. Celeste had furnished the space with lovely antiques and rich fabrics that belied the sense of taste she exhibited in her choice of wardrobe.

She smiled as she noticed Sam's appreciative look. "Nice, huh? I was married a few times. I collected a few nice pieces for the effort."

"You sure did. Where are you from?"

Celeste hesitated before she answered, "Biloxi."

Sam sensed she was lying, but he simply nodded as Celeste sat down on the four-poster bed and patted the spot alongside her. "Sit, Sam," she directed, "you look like you could use a good back rub. Or how about a drink?"

When Celeste reached for a bottle on the nightstand, Sam put out his hand and gently stopped her. "Thanks for the offer, Celeste, but no thanks to both."

Celeste eyed him carefully. "You want *something*, Sam Lerner."

"Yes, I'm actually here to ask you a few questions about Madsen," he replied.

Celeste rolled her eyes and groaned. "Not again. Why can't you and Leon Duval and his backwoods boys just let it be? A hooker drowned, so what's the big friggin' deal?"

"You didn't like her I take it?"

"Didn't say that. But now that you're asking, not really. She got on my nerves with that innocent little girl act. She was no different than the rest of us, only she was hoping to find some sap to take her away from all this. I think she saw *Pretty Woman* twenty times–you know that film where Richard Gere saves Julia Roberts from a life as a call girl? What bullshit!"

"You can't blame her for fantasizing, can you?"

"What's the point? Does it look like we got it so bad? I do this because I have a good time. I make bank, and I have no guilt. After all, professional escorts are more moral than most cops, don't you think?" Celeste jabbed.

"Well, Ma'am, you're probably right," Sam drawled in an expert impersonation of Gary Cooper in *High Noon.*

Celeste laughed. "Besides," she said flirtatiously, "if I was too moral, you wouldn't be decorating my room with your hunky self right now." Celeste reached out to touch Sam's thigh, fixing him with an intense gaze.

Sam gently removed her hand and placed it back on the bed. "Celeste, you seem pretty forthright-"

"You coulda stopped at 'pretty,' " she said, cutting him off.

"That you certainly are. But I need more than that. I need information. Do you know if there was anyone special in Madsen's life? I'm referring to her outside interests more than her 'work' interests."

"I'm perceptive, Sam, and I perceive an unusual interest on your part. You got sucked in by her, too, didn't you?"

"No, I got sucked in by Duval. I used to be a cop in Los Angeles."

"I heard. There are few secrets here at the Hormone Hotel, you know. In answer to your question, Madsen liked several of our johns, but I don't remember their names." She walked over to her vanity, pulled a Marlboro out of the top drawer, and lit up before Sam could get up to offer her a light.

"Do you know who might have given her the expensive perfume, the Dolce & Gabbana Velvet Desire perfume? I see you have some yourself," he added, having already taken a mental photograph of her dressing table.

"You're pretty damn observant," Celeste said. "I've no idea," she said a bit too adamantly, "I bought my own."

Sam watched over Celeste's shoulder as she rearranged her tousled hair in the mirror. "Was Madsen afraid of any of her johns?" he inquired as she primped.

Celeste stopped fidgeting and stared at Sam in the mirror, smoke trailing from her nostrils like dry ice vapors. "How in the hell would I know a thing like that?"

Before he could answer, Celeste turned around to look him in the eyes. "Maybe you shouldn't mess with things that aren't any of your business, Sam. Things could get sticky. You seem to have forgotten our ways down here. Now, if you want me to make you feel good, I can do that. But I don't have time to sit around and talk about a dead hooker all day."

"You seem defensive."

"No, just busy, I'm afraid." Celeste walked to the door and opened it, signaling that their conversation had come to an end. She thrust one hip to the side in an unconscious effort to soften her stance. "It was nice looking at you, Sam Lerner."

Sam was satisfied he had gotten more information than she had intended to give. He stood up and walked past her into the hall. "Thank you for your company, Celeste," he smiled. And you really are pretty," he called back over his shoulder.

He heard the door close quietly, but not until he had turned down the adjacent hall, out of her view.

* * *

Sam was heading for the curved stairway to find Maire when he heard someone quietly speak his name. He turned to see a young woman standing in the hall holding several bags and a bundle of dry cleaning. As she struggled with her packages, her long hair swept against the back of her knees like black billowing curtains. Sam remembered meeting her briefly during his stay at the club.

"Ramona, hello." He grabbed the bundles from her arms and shoved her door open with one foot before following her in. The walls and modest furnishings in the room were every shade of blue he had ever seen. He was instantly depressed.

While he waited for Ramona to take the cleaning from him, Sam moved toward the light. From where he stood, he could see Celeste's room in the adjacent wing of the L-shaped residence. She was sitting in a chair by the window. When she looked up, she noticed Sam observing her. Celeste lit a cigarette and stared at him without expression.

Ramona was looking at him too. "Sorry," he said when he realized she was waiting for him to release her laundry. "I was daydreaming. How have you been, Ramona?"

"Oh, fine, I guess. Have you found out anything about Madsen?" she inquired softly.

"How did you know I was inquiring?"

"Leon Duval told us all you would come around because you wouldn't be able to let it go."

Sam shook his head. "He's right. It's a bad habit. Some things hang on like a case of the clap," Sam grinned. "Ramona, were you friends with Madsen?"

"Sorta. We went to the aquarium together once. It was great–they had a white alligator! And once we went to see that big plantation, Oak Alley. It was real fancy. I thought it musta been neat to live in a mansion like that. But Madsen said the people probably stunk back then 'cause they didn't bathe enough and didn't wear deodorant. And what with those heavy dresses and all-"

Sam gently interrupted her discourse. "Did Madsen ever get phone calls or letters, or meet up with any other friends?"

"No, not really. She might have mentioned one local guy. She said he wanted to get her out of here, maybe get her a big plantation house like Oak Alley. But that was probably just a lot of talk. You ever been to Oak Alley?"

"One time years ago."

"Did you like it?"

"Yes," Sam nodded, "I took my wife there on her first trip to New Orleans." He smiled at the memory of Kira telling a guide that with all those huge trees, someone should have had the sense to build a tree house. After they returned to Los Angeles, Sam had built a tree house for Kira in the big maple out back.

Whenever it rained, they used to climb inside and drink wine and make love. Now he was wishing it had rained more often in Southern California.

"Madsen said your wife died. That's just awful."

"Yes, it was," he nodded.

"I think you've got a real nice dog though," Ramona offered tentatively.

Sam marveled at the way Ramona's thoughts circled and landed scattershot like pesky mosquitoes, but when he saw her sincere expression, he smiled again. "Yes, Beatrice is my best pal. Well, Beatrice and a detective named Joe Bowser back in L.A."

"That's two 'bowsers'!" she grinned.

"I never thought of it that way. But Beatrice's breath is better than Joe's." Ramona giggled and shoved her hair to one side. Sam stared in awe at her long tresses before turning back toward the window.

"Have you talked to Celeste yet?" she asked following his gaze out the window. "She didn't like Madsen."

"Why not?"

"One of Celeste's callers started asking her about Madsen, so Celeste warned Madsen to back off whenever the guy came around."

"Do you know the guy?"

"No, but one day when I was in Madsen's room I saw her staring down into the courtyard at someone. It was on one of those days when you were sleeping here. I couldn't see him too clear, but he was, you know, kinda bulky, and he had dark hair. She seemed repulsed. That's about all I can tell you, 'cept that Madsen said she was being followed, and then she went missing soon after that."

"You sure she wasn't planning a trip?"

"Positive. Other than a few day trips with me, she only took off one night. I remember she took a bus to see some plantation. She had to borrow my suitcase 'cause hers had given up the ghost. She'd seen some real hard times. I heard she was doing street work up in Baton Rouge for quite a while before coming here, but she didn't save nothing up. I've got some stocks," she added proudly as she pulled out an earnings statement addressed to Ramona Slocum. "See here. I plan to earn enough to go back to Slidell and take care of my family."

"Slidell, huh? That's great, Ramona," he said, memorizing her Social Security number out of habit. "So, Madsen didn't ask to borrow your suitcase this last time?"

"Nope."

Sam was wondering why Duval hadn't bothered to fill him in on such important details. "Did you tell Duval about the suitcase, or about the dark haired guy in the courtyard?" he asked.

"No, he didn't ask. So how come you're not staying here anymore?" she demanded as she followed her thoughts around in her head.

"I'm fixing up the family house in Chalmette. Beatrice is home guarding the castle."

"Does it have nice trees?"

"Yeah, real nice."

Ramona smiled and moved closer to the window sill. "Here, take this for your house," she said, offering him a pale pink begonia. "Madsen gave it to me, but I already have one. And I know she thought you were real sweet."

Sam blushed. In all his years as a Los Angeles homicide detective, no one had ever called him 'sweet.' It made him feel soft as hell.

"Thanks, Ramona," he said accepting the plant. A tiny yellow canary was nestled among the blooms. Sam pictured Madsen as she was the last time he saw her, when she had been patiently waiting to talk to him–her "friend." He felt as though he had let her down, and now he wanted to drown the shame of his own failure.

* * *

Sam sat on the plush sofa in the parlor with Maire next to him, her long legs tucked up under her. She stroked his thigh as she nestled against his shoulder.

"How about a bite to eat, chere? I have some lean roast beef and some wonderful French cheese in the pantry."

"No thanks, Maire, maybe later." He stared at the begonia, trying to convince himself there was no need to beat himself up about a heap of shit he couldn't control. He had decided he would satisfy his curiosity about Madsen's death, keep the mother off Maire's back, and then beat it the hell out of town. The charm of the city was wearing thin.

Sam knew if he could sell the farm house for a fair price, he could purchase a place in the Florida Keys where he could fish away his days while Beatrice basked in the sun. They'd both go out in a blaze of lethargic glory. What a plan.

When Maire squeezed his leg, Sam's attention returned to his lovely companion. They had been chatting for three hours, consolidating the events of the past years into concise sentences, sparing the details and offering no excuses or apologies.

Maire had grown up in New Orleans. As a beautiful young woman, she had excellent connections, in spite of the fact that she did not come from upper class lineage or have an advanced education. She left home at sixteen and supported herself by arranging dates between her friends and the wealthy men she met at local jazz clubs. When the girls reported back to her about the gifts and favors they were receiving, she decided it was only fair for her to get a piece of the action. She firmly believed she was providing an age-old service designed to satisfy needs far beyond the physical. To Maire, she had simply become the CEO of a lucrative business.

At twenty-one, Maire had saved enough money to take over the Gentlemen's Club after Miss Rue, the former owner, suffered a heart attack and fell face-first into a plate of sautéed crawdads.

Sam laughed when Maire recalled how medics had to pull crawfish claws out of Rue's buttered turban before wheeling the rotund old madam out on a squealing gurney. While Maire chatted away, Sam's agitation began to subside, and he found himself laughing more easily. As they reminisced about a friendship they had shared since Sam was an innocent teen, he felt his practiced reserve begin to waiver. He tucked his arm around her and pulled her closer. Sam realized he had known Maire a long time, and he had needed her even longer.

"I want you to do me a favor, Sam." Her almond-shaped eyes were studying him with a quiet intensity.

"Anything for you, you know."

"I want you to let Leon Duval do his job. Please get on with your own life, chere. It's not going to help you to keep running from it."

"I have a life. I just have questions about Madsen's death."

"Let it go, Sam. I know what you're doing. You can't keep taking responsibility for dead people."

Maire's words slammed him in the chest. His jaw tightened, as he fought the urge to get up and walk away.

"Talk to me Sam. Please. I've been sitting here patiently, waiting for you to come to me and admit you need a friend. Why are you killing yourself?"

Sam sat in silence, unable to answer. All their lives, Maire had known what his defenses were. And now she knew if he focused on Madsen, he could avoid dealing with his sorrow for the loss of Kira. But Maire wasn't about to let him do that.

"Tell me how Kira died," she whispered.

Sam abruptly pulled away from her. She had done it to him again. She had thrown a curve so hard that it knocked him off base. "I better go home and feed my dog," he said stiffly as he stood up and reached for the begonia Ramona had given him.

Maire slowly rose from the sofa. At six feet, she was able to look him almost eye to eye. Sam noticed the flecks of green in her irises when he met her gaze. The sudden discomfort he felt by their closeness made him feel awkward and shy.

Maire moved in before he could turn away. When she tenderly placed her lips against his, Sam was again caught off guard. He closed his eyes, feeling the warmth of Maire's mouth and the rush of heat to his groin. Then, he kissed her back, hard. Something inside him stirred as his body tried to keep up with his mercurial feelings.

After he kissed her again with a hunger he had long suppressed, he slowly pulled away and walked toward the door. "Car accident," he said over his shoulder as he shoved open the screen. "My wife died in a car accident. She was taking her old VW to get the brakes fixed. I was right behind her in my car. The seatbelt failed, so she smashed her head and tore her face to pieces. It took her three agonizing hours to die. All I could do was stand there and watch."

Sam turned back to Maire. "I should have been driving the VW, Maire. I knew the brakes were shot, but I let Kira drive it because it was uncomfortable for a man my size. Never let it be said that I don't take good care of Sam Lerner." His lungs felt as if they had been punctured, but he somehow made it onto the front porch.

"Chere-" Maire whispered.

Sam left the sound of her voice somewhere in the parlor as he quietly closed the door behind him. He had said it. It hadn't been that hard to say after all. But Kira was still dead, and he couldn't bring her back. He found himself in the sun, staring down at the begonia while the tiny yellow canary appraised Sam Lerner.

Chapter 12

Madsen was falling again, tumbling through the darkness into an airless hole that was pulling her towards the center of the earth. She had discovered what death was. It was being alone in the black abyss while still possessing the senses of the living.

Madsen tried to blink her eyes. She suddenly could see an open mouth. A laugh came out of the mouth, and the assault of the noise made her dizzy. She was looking at the man sitting across the table from her. He smiled and stroked her hand. She asked the waiter for more whiskey sauce for her bread pudding before turning back toward the laugh.

Then a second man joined them. Madsen was afraid of the intruder. She knew him, and she tried to say his name. He ignored her as he poured whiskey, than he demanded she sample the wine. "Drink it," he said menacingly. "Don't be rude." Her date looked away as he tried to hide the fear and sadness in his eyes. Madsen moved her mouth to talk, but she was paralyzed with terror.

Now she closed her eyes, and waited for the image of the men to go away. Then she heard strange voices. The sounds were coming from somewhere outside the black hole that encased her. A ship's horn called from the distance as footsteps pounded the ground nearby.

Suddenly she was moving. Nausea rose in her throat and the smell of bile coated her nose. As she felt her body tip to one side, a cool object fell across her face. Madsen touched it with her lips. A chain, she thought. Then she remembered her necklace. With her tongue, she gathered the oblong silver pendant into her mouth and tried to suck it like a pacifier, but her mouth was too dry.

The thirst in her throat was painful, so she tried to rub her tongue along the top of her mouth, but the dry tissues stuck together causing her to gag. She gagged so hard her head jolted upward into the top of the suffocating box that held her. Her teeth pierced her lip, bathing her mouth in blood. She suckled her own lip like a child at its mother's breast.

Shaking with fear, Madsen tried not to think about how long she would she be in this pit before the worms fed on her body. Perhaps they already had eaten her, which was why she could feel nothing below her neck. Maybe bugs had crawled inside her private parts to punish her evil. She imagined the bugs reproducing inside her body cavity, living inside her deadness.

"Oh God help me," she silently screamed. Holding the pendant in her mouth, Madsen forced her head upward and tried to scratch the wood structure above her so someone would hear her. No one answered. She repeated her desperate movements until she tasted blood from her nose, which she lapped at in a last attempt to cling to life.

Madsen knew she was on the verge of insanity. She begged God to let her brain die, but it stayed alive to torture her. She knew she was falling deeper into the earth where no one could help her. Another scream rose in her consciousness, but it never found a voice. Finally Madsen's mind shattered. As death closed in, she began to babble.

Chapter 13

The sound of rain dancing on the metal roof helped Sam think. He lay on the cot in the old farmhouse with one arm propped under his head. Beatrice lay spread eagle on the floor enjoying the cool air that had been ushered in by a mild gulf storm. As the rain fell gently, it left streaks on the dusty window panes. The remaining sun was nestled low in the sky beneath the incoming fog.

Sam was ill at ease. That day he had placed a call to Leon Duval to try to run down the license plate of the Lincoln that had tailed him. As he suspected, there was no plate registered with the numbers on the tags. Duval also mentioned he had filed the necessary paperwork to exhume Madsen, although he was expecting a losing battle with the judge.

Sam was being pulled into something that wasn't his business, yet he was in too far to turn back. He knew if he wanted answers, it was imperative that he mentally re-create the lost three days after his arrival at Maire's, exhausted and emotionally depleted. As he tried to recall details, he settled into a light sleep, drifting back to Madsen's room.

He remembered getting up several times to relieve his bladder, which kept interfering with his sleep. When he returned, Madsen was wrapped in the yellow robe, and a silver pendant was hanging below her neckline. She was holding a book on screen legends, which was open to a photo of Ava Gardner.

After Sam had crawled back into bed, Madsen talked about how much she loved the movies, and asked if he would go to a nearby movie theater with her that weekend to see a film about a female prostitute in China. She said it would be educational to see what China looks like. When Sam agreed, Madsen bent down to kiss him on the cheek like an excited child. As her pendant brushed against his cheek, Sam noticed that the locket smelled as though it had been dipped in perfume.

Now, on his cot in Chalmette, Sam suddenly snapped his eyes open and looked at the ceiling. The room had grown dark, the moonlight diffused by the fog. Beatrice had changed positions so that her head was resting on his boot. Sam sat up and tried to shake away the effects of his sleep while still grasping at the memories that his sleep had induced.

He pictured Madsen's drawer, the one he had inspected when he met her mother. A book about Hollywood screen legends had been tucked inside under an old sweater. His dream had been an accurate recollection of his time with her. If Madsen had wanted to go to the movies that weekend, then why did she disappear the day he left? And Madsen had told Ramona she was being followed. He scratched his head as he swung his long legs over the edge of the cot and stood up to think more clearly. Suddenly he realized what had been gnawing at the periphery of his consciousness. He flipped on the light and dialed the phone.

"Maire, please," he said when the voice answered.

"I'm sorry, but she's not in. Anything I can do for you, sugar?"

"Will you Get Ramona for me?"

"You're too late," the voice answered, "Ramona's gone."

Sam tried to identify the inflections of the voice over the static of the cordless phone she was using. "Did Ramona leave for good?" he inquired.

"Probably for bad," the woman laughed. "Who knows? Is this Sam Lerner?"

"Hello, Celeste, I thought it was you."

"Come on by for a drink, sugar. We didn't part on such friendly terms, and I'm feelin' a warm spot in my heart for you tonight."

"And why might that be?"

"Because you're not like the others. You don't expect anything."

"Well, thanks, I guess," Sam said. "But I do need something tonight."

"Name it, sweetheart."

"I need information."

"Baby, you're always on the job. What do you need to know now that's keeping you for comin' over to have a good time with me?"

"Tell me about Madsen's silver pendant."

"*Silver plate*," she corrected.

"I know. But it was a strange shape. Did it have some particular meaning to her?"

"Not really. She bought it from some door-to-door salesperson. But she just loved it. She even had that piece of crap engraved with her name. She had cheap taste."

"How come it smelled like perfume?"

"You men sure are dense about women's stuff. The pendant opened, and solid perfume was inside it–a really strong scent."

"What was the scent, Celeste?"

Sam knew the answer before he asked the question, but it was age-old training that made him confirm all the facts. He had smelled the perfume around Madsen's neck, and now he was homing in on his worst suspicion.

"Gardenia."

Sam was mentally elsewhere as her voice trailed off. He remembered falling down in the grass on the levee while trying to find his way in the dark during the pursuit following his dinner at Tujagues. Lying alongside the coffin-like box, he had smelled gardenia through small holes in the wood. He had always had a heightened sense of smell, and the fragrance of Madsen's locket was distinctive.

Were Madsen's remains in the makeshift box? And If Leon and Maire had arranged for her burial at Lafayette Cemetery, why would a coffin containing her remains be unloaded at the water front en route to the cemetery?

* * *

As the hours passed, the winds shifted and the rain turned into a pounding storm. Sam couldn't sleep as he tried to figure out his place in the entire melodrama into which he had somehow stumbled. His constant desire for a drink wasn't helping, so he decided to get dressed and head over to wait for Antoine to open up the restaurant so he could relax over a plate of eggs. After he pulled on his boots, he checked his vintage Timex: 4:00 A.M. Even Antoine would still be asleep.

Sam was heading for the bathroom when he heard a sound at the window. He automatically reached for the baseball bat he used to hit balls for Beatrice. The dog barked loudly as Sam ducked down and made his way toward the wall on his hands and knees, bat in hand. He struggled to control his breathing as he sidled up to the side of the window and pressed his back tightly against the wall.

Beatrice continued to bark, making it difficult for him to identify the sounds outside, but if he hushed the dog, he would give away his position in the room. He grabbed a coat hanger off his desk, braced it between his knees, and untwisted the wire with one hand. Keeping his eye on the window, he used the wire to pull the lamp cord from the socket. The room went dark.

Through the glass, Sam could now see a figure moving in the rain. He quickly assessed the size and shape of the trespasser while Beatrice ran along the wall growling at the prowler's movements.

When the prowler lifted an arm to give a signal, Sam spotted another person standing farther away in the shadows, obscured by rain and fog. As Sam slowly crawled through the rooms, he used Beatrice's growl to keep track of the intruder's position. After he passed through the kitchen, he released the bat from his grasp just long enough to yank his weapon from the drawer.

Sam made it to the front door at the same time footsteps shook the old porch. In one move, Sam flipped the switch to the porch light, yanked open the door, and lowered his weapon. A figure in a wet cloth coat and a clinging scarf blinked in the bright light. "Don't shoot," the voice pleaded. Sam instantly recognized the voice.

"Mrs. Oleyant?" he sputtered as Madsen's mother pulled the drenched scarf from her head. "Who's that with you?"

"Please call me Renee. I'm with a hired hand named Avery. We had to park out in the field 'cause your road is flooded. I couldn't see the house too good. And there's not much moon."

"You could get shot walking outside people's bedrooms in the middle of the night."

"I'll take my chances. I need you to come with me right now."

"Come where? Do you know what time it is?"

"I can read a clock. And I need you to come. Don't ask questions, 'cause it's just something you have to see."

"Mrs. Oleyant, uh, Renee, pardon my suspicious nature, but I am an ex-cop. I don't go anywhere in the middle of the night without asking questions."

"You have no reason to fear me."

"I have no reason to trust you," Sam retorted. He looked at Madsen's mother then at her companion, who had moved closer to the porch. The man had the posture of the elderly. His coat was too large for him and his hat was too small.

He was slight in build, and he literally didn't have the sense to come in out of the rain. Sam decided the threat was minimal.

After he grabbed a hat, he followed the pair across the rapidly flooding field and got in their truck. Even with his weapon still in hand, his apprehension mounted as they made their way through the mud toward the highway.

* * *

The truck Sam was riding in reminded him of some vintage piece out of *The Grapes of Wrath.* So did Renee Oleyant's companion, Avery. Although Sam could barely read the landmarks in the relentless rain, his instincts told him that Avery had turned the truck onto Route 39. They rode without conversation, three abreast, as they headed toward town.

When the lightening began, Sam turned on the radio and tuned it into the local weather station. Above the static he heard a newscaster warning of flash floods and unexpected winds.

As they followed the St. Bernard Highway to St. Claude Avenue and across the Inner Harbor Canal, Sam was surprised to see how quickly the water had risen. It was now framing the edge of the road with a murky blackness.

Avery made a move to avoid a pothole, causing the truck to slide to one side. Sam could feel the heat in his neck as Avery struggled to keep control of the vehicle. Renee stared straight ahead, motionless. When they continued through town into the Garden District, Sam knew he had been correct in his suspicions. They were heading toward the cemetery where Madsen had been buried.

"Couldn't we do this in the morning?" Sam asked, breaking the silence.

When neither answered, Sam studied the driver. Avery was not as old as his posture indicated. Up close, he appeared to be in his late thirties. His shoulders were small, and the curve of his spine was obviously a structural anomaly. Avery held his head forward on his neck as though it were weighted down by a yoke. His hands were large and streaked with dirt. Sam could make out thin but well defined legs beneath Avery's wet trousers. When he turned the wheel, Avery's forearms protruded from his jacket. The man's arms reminded Sam of Popeye. Avery was apparently stronger than he appeared.

Well at least Avery would be of help when the battered truck broke town in the rain, Sam mused. Sam sure as hell wasn't going to push. He had decided he was too pissed at the mystery of this little jaunt to accommodate his two charming hosts, should the occasion arise.

After they pulled up on a side street by the old cemetery, Avery shoved the truck into park. He pressed his body against the door as he struggled to exit against the wind and rain. Sam could barely see Avery as the man trudged through the rain to the cemetery gates. After he shoved the gate of the cemetery open, Avery hunkered in the wind and made his way back to the truck.

"Blew shut," he grunted to no one in particular as he got back in.

"He picked the lock the first time," Renee offered as a terse means of explanation to Sam.

"You two sure know how to entertain," Sam grunted. Renee's posture immediately made him regret the sarcasm he had used to vent his frustration. "So you have accepted that Madsen is dead?" he asked softly.

"No, but I came to the city of the dead to see for myself, Mr. Lerner. Now I want you to see. Avery, please move the truck somewhere less obvious and join us."

She got out of the car and signaled for Sam to come. He sighed and followed her along the deserted street to the gate. When the lightening ripped through the black sky, it illuminated ghoulish scenery eerily backlit by heavy rain.

Vaults for the dead lined the grounds in endless rows, perched on the earth's surface so the bayou country would not regurgitate its corpses. Sam had heard reports of bodies that had been buried years ago rising up during past floods to float down deluged streets. Although he understood the practicality of above-ground tombs, they evoked images of bodies lying around in some half-dead state. This was definitely not his choice of places to be during an unforgiving storm.

When Avery joined them, he pushed the gate open enough for them to pass through. "Hey, buddy," Sam cautioned, "we could get arrested for this. And maybe you haven't noticed, but there's lightening striking down all over the place. I suggest you drop that metal pipe you're carrying unless you have a vault picked out here for your own resting place."

"We walk from over that way," Avery mumbled. He and Renee stepped forward together as if in response to some inaudible cue. After a moment, Sam wordlessly trailed after them.

They made their way down a row of elaborate tombs, each one more artistically carved and ornamented than the next. The beam from Avery's flashlight bounced erratically off the carved statues giving each a brief, ghostly life.

Sam shuddered at the macabre images. The water soaked through his boots as he walked. He tilted his face upward and parted his lips to allow the water to moisten his dry mouth.

When Renee slipped in the mud, Sam grabbed her arm to give her support. He was surprised at her resilience as she stood straight and forged ahead. Avery kept his bent frame low against the rain, the light occasionally reflecting off his face.

"I think we're breaking a few laws here, folks," Sam reminded them, expecting no result. And he got none. Avery and Renee Oleyant continued to make their way over the decaying terrain to the oldest and most untended corner of the cemetery.

"It's the pageant of ghouls," Sam muttered under his breath as they came upon an area of the cemetery where the tombs were piled atop one another to conserve space. Many were very old and had no grave markers, and the care given to this particular area of the cemetery seemed nonexistent. Weeds had grown high between the stone vaults, and many tombs had actually slid off their foundations. Renee stopped in front of an old vault and stared into the darkness.

"Give Mr. Lerner the light, Avery," she ordered her companion.

Sam took the light and approached the grave. As he got closer, he noticed that the stone frontispiece had been pried off and cast aside in the wet weeds.

"You did this by yourself?" Sam asked. The man shrugged and nodded. Sam then turned to Renee and pointed the light near enough to see her face. "Madsen's grave?" Renee set her jaw, but said nothing.

"I'm getting tired of my own voice here," he grunted. Sam held the light steady as he moved closer to the tomb. A broken tree branch had fallen against the tomb opening, and a flood of water was draining off the tree into the open vault. He shoved the leaves away from his face and peered in.

"What in hell-?" he gasped.

Evidently Avery had also pried open the inner coffin. Sam aimed the light inside. The torrents of rain had begun to fill the coffin, causing its contents to shift suddenly. Sam let out a yelp and stepped back involuntarily. Losing his footing, he fell into the weeds, where he sat for a moment before getting to his feet.

Renee was crouched near a stone marker lying on the ground. Sam walked over and focused the light until he could make out the engraving. **Madsen**

Cassaise was carved in small, upright letters. Renee ran her graceful fingers along the letters that formed her daughter's name. "Madsen Cassaise. It should say 'Oleyant,' like her mama."

"Maire didn't know," Sam said gently. Renee grunted and then stepped away from the stone as if it were tainted.

When Sam glanced down again, he detected a small white object near the headstone. In the dim light, he could see a card made of thick, fine quality stationery now wet and muddy from the weather. He picked it up and carefully tucked it inside his shirt, flat against his chest.

When Sam finally went back to the tomb, he took in a deep breath. He looked around to locate Avery, feeling some inexplicable need to keep track of the guy. Then Sam shined the light in the grave once again.

The wind and the rising water were causing the body to move around like laundry in a washing machine. Just as Sam paused to wipe the pounding rain from his eyes, one side of the damaged casket gave way due to water load. The body suddenly shifted, and the right hand of the corpse lurched upward as if its owner were performing a benediction.

Sam fought his urge to beat a path back to the truck. Instead he focused the light on the protruding hand. It bore a ring with an insignia: United States Air Force Academy.

Sam didn't know whose dead body he was staring down at, but the decedent was most certainly was a male. Sam looked at Renee, whose face reflected his own thoughts: So where in the hell was Madsen?

Chapter 14

Sitting in the garden of Maire's Gentlemen's Club was always a pleasant experience for Sam. He breathed in the scent of Maire's roses as she bent to clip off the few blooms that had survived the storm. Creeping honeysuckle and bright purple morning-glories climbed the walls while music drifted into the courtyard from within the house, accompanied by occasional bursts of laughter.

Sam was stretched out on a wrought iron chaise lounge, comfortably tucked into its cushions. He was happy to be dry and back from the dead. He stared at a bottle of Cuervo Gold Tequila on the table. Leon Duval was offering no assistance to Sam's willpower. Duval had left a note and the bottle of their old college poison in the Shelby sometime that morning before Sam's return from the cemetery. "Thanks for the advice," was all Duval had written on the note, referring to Sam's counsel to start the paperwork required to exhume Madsen's body.

"Yeah, well you may not be thanking me once you get wind of an illegally exposed grave and a missing body," Sam thought.

As he sighed and reached for a pitcher of iced tea, it occurred to him how exhausted he was. By the time Renee Oleyant and her hulking companion had delivered Sam back to his house in Chalmette, it had been almost daylight. Guichard Canal had flooded, making it difficult for them to return to the farm. And the road on Sam's property was also impossible to distinguish, so Sam had been forced to wade the last mile.

On the way back, Renee Oleyant informed Sam she had gone to the cemetery with the intention of taking her daughter back to Picayune. She wanted Madsen buried face down according to voodoo ritual so her daughter wouldn't be possessed by another spirit. She claimed she had already explained this to Leon

Duval, who had vehemently protested. Duval claimed Madsen had been given a fine burial and insisted if Renee loved Madsen, she'd let her rest in peace "no matter which way she was facing."

He shook his head at the thought of Duval's lack of diplomacy. Although Sam had informed Renee that Duval had finally decided to obtain an order to exhume, she had remained determined to handle matters herself. After Sam returned from the cemetery, unnerved and baffled by his romp with the dead, he had cleaned up and headed for the Gentlemen's Club hoping Maire could provide the answers he needed to make sense of everything.

When he looked up, Maire was staring at him. He knew he would never get tired of looking at her. "Good morning," he smiled. She was a welcome respite after his bizarre evening.

"Hi, handsome, what's going on? Your thoughts are blowing across your face like autumn leaves. You're not just here for a hearty breakfast, are you, chere?" She tipped her head and smiled as she waited for a response.

Sam found himself grinning, which was something that came easily for him whenever he was around her. He had met her when he was still in high school, not long after his father had plunged into the canal in a fatal drunk-driving accident.

Sam was living at the farm house in Chalmette at the time and was determined to make enough money to stay there, so one night soon after the accident, Sam took the old Ford truck into town to look for a part-time job.

He was applying for work in a bar on Bourbon Street when he first saw Maire. At twenty-one, she was proud and confidant as she swept through the room, towering over many of the patrons as she made her way to the piano. "Play me some Cole Porter," she drawled to the pianist, "nice and easy-like." Sam became an instant fan of Cole Porter. The fact that Sam had an erection from watching her walk did little to discourage his assessment of the effects of Porter's music. Or of Maire Girod.

Sam was too shy to approach her, but he did follow her back to the house on Ursulines that night where he parked his truck and waited. He didn't know what his intent was, he just knew he had to meet her. Now Sam smiled at the memory. That night he saw a number of men come and go until he finally figured out what was going on. He didn't get up the nerve to knock on the door until three o'clock in the morning. She answered.

"I was wondering when you'd come in," she told him. "I was getting awfully tired of waiting. I'm Maire."

"I know, I asked at the bar. I'm Sam. I don't have any money."

"Then what is it you want?"

"Nothing," Sam answered, embarrassed by his lack of verbal skills. "I was just sitting there, and I guess, well I guess I just don't have any reason to go home."

"Were you planning on sitting in your truck all night?"

"I don't sleep much."

"I see." Maire stared at him for a moment before she opened the door wider and gestured for him to come in. "I was about to make myself a sandwich. Keep me company?"

Sam followed her into the kitchen without saying another word. After enough brandy to overcome his shyness, Sam talked with Maire for hours. That night they became friends, and Sam soon discovered that in many respects Maire was only as old as he. She had grown up too quickly, her childhood stolen by an older relative who had been a trusted father-figure. That's when she left a home that no longer provided comfort or safety. That first night they met, they both needed laughter and friendship to fill the void each was experiencing in their separate lives.

Sam had always had to struggle with his libido whenever Maire was around. She teased him, and he flirted and jokingly begged, but their relationship was too necessary to both of them to threaten it with the complications of sex. Both feared losing their friendship, and neither wanted to lose anything else in life. Sam's friends always assumed Maire was servicing him, despite his denials. He found it impossible to explain to them something he didn't understand himself.

In later years after they parted ways, Sam regretted not having had that intimacy with Maire. Now, as he stood before her wanting answers in a game he didn't choose to be playing, he wondered why the paths in his life kept bringing him back to this woman.

"You're staring at me, Sam," she whispered.

"You should be used to that," he said quietly. "Your roses are looking real fine."

"Sam Lerner, you didn't come here to admire my roses. Your face is present and accounted for, but your eyes haven't even noticed that my kimono is transparent in the sun. You, my love, have got a major distraction going on."

"Don't think I didn't notice, babe. I just can't get a scene from last night out of my mind."

"Where were you? Leon Duval said you weren't there when he dropped by your place at six this morning. I guess Beatrice has taken to growling at him."

"So have I. So you've talked to our decadent friend already this morning?"

"He checks in occasionally. He was calling to make sure I was harboring no trouble makers."

Sam smiled ruefully. "Bullshit, Maire, I know Leon Duval is on the take. You have to pay that smiling Bubba asshole to keep your business up and running, don't you?"

"I'll have none of that language here, Sam Lerner. I run a respectable god-damn gentlemen's club," she grinned "And I have no idea what you mean by 'on the take' regarding our mutual friend."

"Right. I've been gone a while, but I sense Baby Huey has his hand in more than one pocket."

"Sam, don't be mean. I know Leon Duval can be annoying, but he's harmless."

"What in the hell has happened to this town? A police captain is not sup-posed to be harmless!" Sam playfully threw an ice cube at Maire then watched as it slid between her breasts, following the path of least resistance downward over her luminous skin to parts unknown to Sam. Sam vicariously enjoyed the ice cube's chosen route to mysterious places he had long visualized in great detail.

Maire squealed as the ice cooled her. "Why are you so impatient with him, you cantankerous man?"

Sam had been wondering that himself. Since his return to New Orleans, he had been constantly short with Leon Duval, although the big oaf seemed to be trying to do him a favor by distracting Sam with some minor police business.

But ever since their college football days, Duval had been adept at bend-ing the rules. By good-ol'-boying-it to the top, Duval had become one of the youngest police captains in New Orleans' history. Playing dirty was something Sam found distasteful. However, although Duval did whatever it took to win, Sam knew he always looked out for his team. Sam decided maybe he needed to cut Duval some slack and get back on the same team. After all, someone had to help him find Madsen's body.

While Sam considered the possibilities of teaming up with Duval, Maire draped her long body alongside him in the chaise. "Fill me in on last night, love."

"We've got a problem, Maire," he explained, as he slid an arm under her neck. "I was at the cemetery where Madsen is buried. I went with Mrs. Oleyant and a strange sidekick of hers."

"Go on."

"And Madsen wasn't there."

Maire bolted upright. "What are you saying?"

"The grave was open, and Madsen wasn't there."

"Not there?" she repeated. "What do you mean by 'not there'?"

"I mean exactly what it sounds like. There was a male corpse in the grave that bore the headstone with Madsen's name on it. Have you been out there to make sure the stone was on the correct grave site?"

"No, I just paid for it and told them to deliver it."

"You were the one who identified the body, weren't you?"

"Yes, I was."

"Any chance of a mistake, love?"

"I'd be the last person to mistake a man for a woman, Sam!"

Sam laughed at her expression. "Well, are you sure the person in the coffin at the funeral was the same one you had identified?"

"I can only assume. It wasn't really a funeral—just a gravesite blessing. The casket was already sealed." Maire suddenly leaned forward and grabbed the bottle of Cuervo. After she pulled off the lid, she took a long swig then passed it to him. He held the bottle, but didn't drink.

Sam took a deep breath as she brushed her long legs against his and then laid her head against his chest. He hadn't realized how badly he had been looking for an excuse to hold her again. Maire caressed his arm, outlining his muscle with her fingers. Then she reached for the bottle and chugged again.

Sam wondered if he should slow her down. "I haven't seen you drink directly from a bottle since we were kids, Maire."

"Some things require expediency," she sighed as she draped one arm over her eyes.

He pulled her close enough to stroke her elegant neck with his hand. "Darlin', I need to talk to Ramona. Is she back yet?"

"I don't think she's coming back. She left two days ago. She just packed some things and left town."

"She didn't leave a note or say anything about leaving?"

"No, but I'll let you know if she returns or calls. Should we be worried?" At Sam's silence, Maire took another long drink. It was obvious she was rattled. When she pulled her mouth away, the tequila ran down the side of the bottle.

"Excuse me, Maire, but I need to set up a visit with the coroner."

While Sam dialed, he noticed a silhouette of someone watching him from behind one of the long shutters that covered the French doors. Before the person retreated, Sam got a quick glimpse of blond hair. He was sure Maire had noticed too, because she was reaching for the bottle again.

Sam was convinced Maire was afraid of something, but he couldn't put the pieces together. He leaned down, took the bottle from her, and kissed her forehead. "Don't worry. I'll take care of you, chere," he assured her, slipping into the old Southern patois.

"Thanks, Sam, but I'm not sure you can," she whispered. Sam followed her gaze to the door. Celeste was no longer there.

Chapter 15

Coroner Malcolm Wilson sat across from Sam rubbing his rheumy eyes with a closed fist. In Sam's opinion, the coroner smelled worse than some of the deads he had bagged back in L.A. Either the coroner had been lapping up a little of the preserving fluids in the lab, or the guy was toasted. The eyes were definitely a clue the old guy liked his booze.

"I don't know what could have happened, Mr. Lerner," Wilson told Sam between belches. "I'm talking to you out of courtesy of course, as you have no jurisdiction in these parts."

"I no longer have any jurisdiction in any parts," Sam shrugged.

"But you introduced yourself as a friend of Leon Duval."

"As I said, I'm helping out at his request."

"I see." When Wilson leaned back in his chair and scratched his temple, an ill-fitting toupee readjusted itself to the coroner's undersized head.

Wilson suddenly launched into a coughing fit. While waiting for the hacking to subside, Sam studied the man carefully. The brown spots on the coroner's hands and the sallow cast to his skin indicated advanced liver damage. Sam suspected that the excessive bloat in Wilson's face was indicative of steroid treatment for something pernicious. He grimaced as Wilson swallowed a mass of sputum before continuing.

Although Wilson stared at a folder of paperwork he was holding, he didn't really appear to be focused. "So, Mr., uh, Lerner, as I said, we released the girl to Whitaker's funeral home. I know nothing more." Keeping his thumb between the pages, Wilson closed the file and shot a lifeless smile at Sam.

"I understand the body was here for only a week," Sam prodded.

Wilson made a show of checking his notes again as he tried to loosen the phlegm in his throat. "That's correct."

"Do you usually take only a week to try to locate relatives?"

"Frankly, Mr. Lerner, I resent your implication, even if you and Duval are friends. We sometimes have a body in here forty days before we give up and send it to potter's field. In this case, however, it was justifiable to expedite the matter."

"I'm not following."

Wilson sighed, looked at his watch, and then made a show of reading from the file. "Ms. Maire Girod, the deceased's employer, was able to identify Miss Cassaise's body. The deceased had assured Ms. Girod that she had no living relatives anywhere. With that information, which was corroborated by our own police captain, Leon Duval, I released the victim's body. Is that so difficult to understand?"

"I think I get it," Sam said, ignoring Wilson's sarcasm. "And you're quite sure the death was the result of a drowning accident?"

"I have no doubt."

"No indications of struggle?

"No."

"Any marks indicating foul play?"

"Absolutely not," Wilson snapped as he looked over the file. "I would have brought such evidence to Captain Duval's attention. Now I really must get back to work."

Before Wilson could rise, Sam stood up and leaned across the desk, holding his face just inches from the coroner's. He slipped one finger into the file where Wilson's thumb still separated the pages. "You don't seem to understand the importance of the information I am seeking, sir," Sam said with steely politeness.

Wilson turned his face away from Sam. "Let it be! The woman was just a hooker who drowned. And you have no official business here, so I must ask you to leave. We already have more work than we can handle down here."

Wilson began to cough again, this time more violently. He dragged a well-used handkerchief out of his lab coat to stifle his gagging. As the coughing spell continued, Wilson lost his patience and kicked the file cabinet. Then, in a gesture that struck Sam as oddly surreal, Wilson apologized to the file cabinet.

Sam feared Wilson was either going to depart from reality altogether or drop dead. It was a toss-up as to what might come first. He stared at Wilson, who was folding his damp handkerchief into an impossibly small square.

Wilson spoke again as though he were addressing his hankie. "We're overworked enough without some Los Angeles cop sticking his nose in our business and taking up valuable time. And we don't even make enough money to buy two-ply toilet paper. Imagine that! That shit they put in the bathroom is rough enough to scrape tartar off a dog's teeth. I didn't become a coroner to have to rub my ass raw. I'm a doctor, for chrissake, and I-"

Before Wilson could finish his tirade, Sam startled the dissipated coroner by flipping the paper file open to the page where his finger was still serving as a bookmark. He stared down at the page before looking back up at Wilson. Madsen's name was at the top of the page. The rest was blank.

"Impressive records," Sam sneered. "No wonder your office has received so many complaints."

"This is all I can manage, Sorry, but our computer system has been on the fritz for months. We lost a lot of data. I told you we need help."

"So everything you told me was from memory?" Sam demanded.

"No, I had a file, but I misplaced it. I had photos and all the proper documentation. I'm sure it's just misfiled somewhere. That's embarrassing for a man in my position to admit."

"And no one else here knows about this case?" Sam asked as he thumbed through the file of blank pages.

"No, I've been without an assistant in the front office for some time. I thought I could handle it all while interviewing prospective employees, but I admit I was careless," he said contritely as he wiped his mouth with the back of his hand. "I never expected a routine drowning to come back and bite me in the ass. And that's all it was. I assure you, it was a routine drowning."

"Thanks, Wilson." Sam snapped the folder shut and reached for his copy of the New Orleans Times Picayune, which he had placed on the cluttered desk. "I'm sure we'll speak again. Maybe you should get some rest."

"I suppose you think I'm quite unprofessional compared to those celebrity coroners back in Los Angeles, don't you Mr. Lerner?"

"We've got some dodgy ones there, too. Apparently you didn't follow the O.J. case." Sam shot the coroner a wry smile.

"Well, thanks for not embarrassing me further, Mr. Lerner. But please don't come around here again."

"Don't worry, Wilson. I'll only be back if there's good reason to continue our interview." Sam noticed that Wilson's face remained as stiff as his clientele.

* * *

After Sam left the coroner's office, he turned the corner of the hallway and pulled a small notebook out of his pocket to jot down a few notes:

1. No file.

2. Wilson is covering up something.

3. AND WHO IN THE HELL TOLD HIM I'M FROM LOS ANGELES?

Sam shoved the notebook back in his pocket. After he looked around to make sure the coroner was not watching, he stepped into a small room and pulled the door closed behind him. While he waited, he stared down at the telephone on the desk. Within seconds, the red light came on. "Right on cue," Sam muttered.

He hesitated before quietly lifting the receiver. When he pressed the phone to his ear, he could hear the phlegm-heavy voice of Malcolm Wilson. "I'll hold," Wilson was saying to someone.

A voice finally picked up the call on the other end. "Yes?" the voice said.

"Sam Lerner was here," Malcolm announced, then he abruptly hung up. Within seconds, the other line went dead. But Sam was sure he had recognized the voice of the woman who had answered Wilson's call.

* * *

After Sam hung up the phone, he glanced around the cluttered room. From inside the pages of his newspaper, he retrieved the card which he had found the preceding night in the mud near Madsen's grave. He had considered handing it over to Leon Duval, but he wanted to check it out himself first, because Duval had become the black hole of information.

Sam had flattened the large card between two sections of newspaper so the paper would absorb any excess moisture. Most of the writing on the short note was mud-stained and nearly impossible to read.

Sam switched on an x-ray light box he had spotted on his way in. As he held the card up to the light, he strained to make out the details. He could see ballpoint pen indentations in the quality card stock, but the grime that had collected in the light etching further obscured the words. Sam could decipher only four words: "sorry" and "take care of."

In the bottom right corner of the card was another figure. Sam turned the card in several directions to be certain of what he was seeing. Although the mud stain had seeped into the corner of the card, the paper had not absorbed as much of the moisture in that area due to the wax residue from a yellow crayon.

He studied the shape of the yellow area, which had been outlined with dark, and apparently indelible, ink. Sam paused when he finally realized what he was looking at. Someone had drawn a small yellow canary on the card before placing it on the grave where Madsen's body should have been safely at rest.

Chapter 16

Louis Santos leaned against his rented Lexus and took a final pull off his Esplendido. As he tossed the butt on the ground, he continued to watch the window on the second floor of Maire's Gentlemen's Club. Ursulines Avenue was as dark and quiet as he had expected it to be at midnight on a Tuesday evening.

He checked his slicked back hair in the side-view mirror of the car. He had switched cars knowing the cop from Los Angeles would now be on the lookout for him. Fortunately Louis had a dealer friend who owed him big favors, so car exchanges required little more than a phone call. The Lexus had been delivered within an hour, and the Lincoln was receiving a new paint job.

Louis swallowed a mint before pulling a toothpick from his pocket. He picked at a hole in a back molar while he waited. Just as he was losing his patience, he saw the curtain in the front window move slightly. Within minutes, his date stepped out onto the front porch.

Louis watched with mounting excitement as she closed the door and walked toward him. Even though the temperatures had been less punishing in the past few days, he was sweating. Each time she took a step, her hips swayed seductively. Louis felt his excitement growing.

When she reached the car, he placed one hand on her elbow and guided her to the passenger side. Her flesh felt so soft he had to control his urge to run his hand up under the sleeve of her black crepe dress. As she slipped into the seat, he bent closer to suck in her exotic fragrance. Louis unconsciously licked his lips.

"Do you plan to take me for a late supper first?" she asked coquettishly.

"Anything you'd like."

"Perhaps some music?"

"Perhaps."

As Louis slid into the driver's side, he looked over at her, half enjoying the torment of his libido. "Why do you hold me off like this, always wanting me to choose one of the other girls for release?" he whined between heavy breaths.

"You got too rough last time. Bruises are bad for business. I'm testing you to see if you can control yourself." She smiled seductively then reached out to stroke his leg. "Maybe if you're good-"

"I *have* been good, honey!"

"Yes, the other girls tell me you've been more 'subdued' lately."

He smiled then looked away. "I have indeed, sugar, because I want *you*. I am following your orders to restrain my, uh, tendencies." Louis turned on the engine then paused. "Oh, I almost forgot," he said as he reached into his pocket. "Here's that little item you requested." Louis leaned closer and pressed the object into her palm.

She nodded as she inspected his offering. In the glare of the streetlight, she could see that the clasp that secured the locket was broken, thus allowing the sweet smell of gardenia to emanate from the perfumed pendant. The necklace looked as fragile as the neck from which it had been violently torn.

"Nice work," she whispered. She dropped it into her purse then stared out into the night.

Chapter 17

Sam sat at his desk listening to the recorded message and nervously running his hands through his dark hair. He needed a copy of Charlie Biscay's customer list fast. But Charlie's home phone had apparently been disconnected, and the floral shop he owned was closed. But why would Charlie close the shop mid-week, Sam wondered? He placed the phone back on its cradle and slid the mud-stained note card back into his pocket.

Sam was already in an agitated state, and this new development was not helping. Charlie Biscay had been his friend since college when Charlie was still struggling to hide the truth about his sexual preferences. One day Sam had unexpectedly dropped by Charlie's apartment to borrow a camera when he saw a series of intimate photos of male nudes in Charlie's dark room.

Although Sam said nothing, Charlie later admitted he had expected the incident to end their friendship. But when Sam continued to invite Charlie to hang out with him and Duval and the other locals, Charlie's devotion to Sam became permanently cemented.

Over the years they had kept in touch via mail or phone, so Sam was sure Charlie would not pull up stakes without letting him know where he was. And because of Charlie's illness, Sam now feared the worst.

Sam checked his watch. It would have to wait. He was scheduled to meet with Leon Duval at Whitaker's Funeral Home in half an hour. Sam grinned as he recalled stopping by police headquarters to tell Duval about the little problem of an open grave and a missing body. He hadn't seen Duval sputter like that in years. Sam had decided to share the information in order to gauge Duval's reaction. Interesting, he noted.

When Duval got over the shock, he called Whitaker's Funeral Home at Sam's insistence and set up an appointment. Duval also agreed not to bring charges against Renee Oleyant and her skulking companion if Sam could convince the woman to return to Picayune and allow the police to sort out the complications.

After Sam left the station, he dropped back by Maire's place to see if Ramona had checked in. She hadn't. Sam knew he needed some inside help, but something in his gut told him to run his own investigation for now if he wanted answers.

When Sam returned home, he immediately called Los Angeles to enlist the help of his cop friend Joe Bowser in contacting authorities in Slidell, Ramona's hometown. He gave Joe as much information as he could about Ramona, including the last four digits of the social security number, which he remembered from the stock certificates she had proudly shown him. Sam instructed Joe to leave Ramona a message that he needed to speak with her immediately. He also told Joe to warn Ramona not to relay any information through Duval or the New Orleans Police Department. Until he had a handle on what was going on, he planned to play it close to the vest.

* * *

When Sam pulled into the mortuary parking lot, he immediately spotted Leon Duval. Duval was standing next to his unmarked vehicle creating a sequoia-like shadow, and he appeared to be broiling in a cloud of smoke that billowed from the open car door.

When Sam walked closer, he spotted a woman sitting in the front seat of the car smoking a cigarette and reading *Star Magazine*. Sam gestured to the woman and grinned, "Official business, I presume?"

"Got that right," Duval laughed as he slammed the door shut and clapped Sam on the back. "Linny left me 'cause she hated being a cop's wife. So I'm taking care of Leon-business."

"Fair enough. Who's the bimbo du jour?"

"Dagmar. Helluva name, eh? Makes me horny just sayin' it."

Sam laughed and glanced at Dagmar again. Her eyes were glued to a photo of Cher as she absently tried to toss her cigarette out the door, which was now closed. Sam and Duval tried not to laugh as Dagmar suddenly started flopping around in her seat like a speared tuna in an effort to retrieve the burning butt.

"I've seen halibut die with more dignity," Sam smirked as they headed into the funeral home. When Sam stepped through the door, the distinct blend of embalming fluid, deodorizer and perfume took him back to the days in St. Tammany when as teens both he and Duval had worked in the local funeral home. Sam remembered how they were nearly fired for laughing at inopportune moments. For him, it was a nervous response to the macabre situations they often encountered. These days Sam was seldom bothered by corpses, but the heavy solemnity of funeral homes still rattled him.

Duval stopped to peer into a coffin. "Nice make-up job. Remember the time I was told to make-up that old fairy, Pete Hardison?"

Sam's mind flashed back to the time he saw Duval with a photo and a lipstick tube in hand, hovering over the deceased's body. Duval had created a jewel bedecked corpse who resembled the preserved mother in *Psycho*. Sam had laughed so hard he feared Hardison, puckered up and pissed-off, would come back to kick them both in the ass.

Now, with Pavlovian timing, Sam could feel a familiar nervous response welling up in his throat just as Donald Whitaker, Director of Funeral Services, entered the room.

When Duval spun around to greet Whitaker, Sam noticed that Duval's mouth was contorted as he tried to suppress the same nervous laughter Sam was struggling to control. The big lug looked like a lunatic.

"Excuse me?" Whitaker said as a strange sound escaped Sam's lips. Sam looked down at his feet and took in a few deep breaths.

Duval contritely made the introductions. "Whitaker, this is Sam Lerner. Just ignore his tics. He has acute asthma." With that, Sam had to make an immediate exit to the men's room.

As he stood in a stall laughing, he realized it had been a while since he had really laughed freely. Not since before Kira died. Perhaps it was fitting that his emotions surfaced in a mortuary. Maybe he was coming full circle after all.

When he stepped out of the stall, a young man of about eighteen was standing by the sink. The kid checked Sam out in the mirror as he washed his hands.

"Is something wrong, son?"

"No," the kid grinned sheepishly, "I just heard you having an awfully good time in there. I thought maybe you were some kind of a weirdo."

"Don't worry, I'm not dangerous."

"If you say so," the kid said dubiously as he picked up a notebook. "Well, I got a stiff to stuff."

"So you work here?"

"Of course. You think I hang out here for the girls?"

"I hope not. Can you answer a few questions? I'm a detective," Sam added, stretching the limits of the title.

"Cool. Whattya wanna know?"

"How long have you worked here?"

"A week."

"Damn, I was hoping you could remember a particular dead, er, 'deceased' that was sent here a few weeks back. It was a young woman, drowning victim."

"That would be Jared. I'm Jeff. Jared was working then. But he wouldn't remember. He can't remember nothing. He's a junkie, man."

"Do you know where I could find him?"

"He's outta here. They fired his ass for shooting up and then sleeping in somebody's coffin. Creepy, huh?"

"I hope the coffin was unoccupied," Sam grunted, fighting the urge to laugh again. He decided that funeral homes didn't bring out the best in him. "How do you keep track of your, uh, inventory?"

Jeff, eager to prove himself more reliable than his predecessor, pulled open the notebook. "We're supposed to keep the information in this book. It tells the name of the stiff, the family, what kind of box they order, and where the stiff is going to be planted."

"May I please take a look?" When Sam reached for the notebook, several catalogues fell to the floor.

"Help yourself, man," Jeff said as he bent over to retrieve the catalogues. "Detective work must be cool, huh?"

"Yeah, cool," Sam agreed absently as he flipped through the computerized order sheets. He was ready to give up until he noticed Jeff clutching a hand written order page that had fallen out of a catalogue. The name MAIRE GIROD was scrawled at the top of the form.

Sam snatched the paper from Jeff. The order blank listed two sets of numbers and three words: HEADSTONE: MADSEN CASSAISE.

"What do the numbers mean?"

Jeff glanced down then pointed to the first set of numbers. "That's indicates the style of coffin," he explained. "I recognize that one. It's the cheapest – just a wooden container. It's the kind we use mostly for the unclaimed stiffs."

"What do the other numbers mean?"

"Serial number off the casket."

Sam stared at the number. 585911. Ironic, he thought–the last three numbers were 911, a cry for help. He handed the paper back to the young assistant and patted him on the back. "Thanks kid, and be sure not to take your work home with you."

* * *

Sam returned to the mortuary sitting room just as Duval was sizing up the elaborate red velvet curtains and green furniture. "This decor is downright whorehouse festive," Duval blurted to Whitaker before turning to Sam. "Sammy, Whitaker here tells me how the mix-up with the girl's remains probably occurred. Apparently a number of headstones were simultaneously transported. Some druggie who was helping out here must have switched two of them accidently while he was tweaked out. Ms. Cassaise is in another tomb out there, but nonetheless, she has been properly laid to rest."

"How many headstones could possibly have been sent over there at one time?"

"Quite a few. Lots of people die every day, Mr. Lerner."

"Yours must be the most trafficked mortuary in New Orleans, in spite of the recent reports of gross negligence. Yes, I did my research, sir."

Whitaker's face flushed with embarrassment. "Well, the young man responsible is no longer with us. And I personally supervised correction of the damage done to the grave that was opened by that crazy mother. We have the coffin here, and we'll inter the man again upon completion of repairs. It may take us a while to locate the girl, however, we will begin the process immediately and then put the headstones in the appropriate locations."

"The man's family must be irate," Sam said, fishing for information.

"The man that Oleyant woman dug up was never identified, so they'll be no problem there."

Sam noticed that Whitaker was perspiring. "Really?" Sam pressed. "An Air Force Academy grad couldn't have been too hard to identify."

"Huh?" Whitaker and Duval both said at the same time.

"The man in Madsen's grave was in the Academy." Sam saw Whitaker's face turn the color of the drapes. He also sensed Duval getting a bit edgy himself. "He had on a class ring."

"I think you're mistaken, Mr. Lerner," Whitaker argued. "When I went out there to assess the damage, I didn't see a ring on the remains."

"I'm a detective. I know what I saw, Mr. Whitaker."

Duval scratched his head. "I believe ya,' Sammy. But maybe someone stole the ring before they brought the body* back here. Maybe even that crazy mother and her grave-digging sidekick. But the dead guy sure doesn't need it. Regardless, the body was still unclaimed. No relatives. So let's not waste our time with details."

"Of course, no details," Sam said sarcastically. "So Mr. Whitaker, tell me how this airman crawled into the wrong vault."

"He didn't, as you so delicately put it, 'crawl into the wrong vault,' Mr. Lerner. The girl was ready for transport, and then the dismissed employee placed the gentleman on the transport vehicle in an identical coffin, along with several others containing unclaimed deceased. His coffin was simply placed in the wrong location with the wrong headstone. You can understand the confusion when all the lids are down."

"Of course, easy mistake."

Whitaker winced at the sarcasm in Sam's comment. "Captain Duval here has assured me that our error will be excused because the perpetrator of such gross negligence has been terminated, and because we are rectifying the situation. Now, if you two will excuse me, I must tend to business."

"I'd like to take a quick look at the airman, if you don't mind," he said to Whitaker's back. "You said you brought him here?"

Whitaker spun around to stare at Sam. "I did," Whitaker answered tersely, "but the coffin has been resealed." Sam was impressed by how Whitaker could speak without moving his face.

"I just want to make sure everything has been taken care of properly after such a crude form of disinterment."

Whitaker looked at Duval for approval. Duval nodded then led Sam to the back of the mortuary as Whitaker stalked off.

They stepped into a preparation room where a number of open and closed coffins were propped up on pedestals for easy access. Jeff was busy trying to fit a shoe on a corpse when they entered.

"Which one is the one that was disinterred?" Duval asked.

After Jeff pointed out the plain coffin, Sam walked slowly around it. The coffin was the cheapest kind used for charity burials, yet the finish was much smoother than the coffin shaped box he had come upon by the levee. And there were no holes along the side. He ran his fingers along the edges and underneath as far as he could reach.

"What are you doing, buddy?"

"Just want to make sure it's well sealed. I feel real bad about what happened."

"Yeah, helluva freakin' encore for a dead guy."

Sam grunted and crouched down to look up under the part of the coffin that extended out over the pedestal. He instantly found what he was looking for. "Jeff, are you positive this is the one they brought in this morning?" Sam asked as he ran one finger over a small metal plate affixed to the bottom of the casket.

"I'm positive, man. It had a shitload of water in it. We gutted the thing–the box I mean, not the dead guy. Than we fixed it up and stuck him back in."

Sam stared up at the metal plate. He could just make out the serial number engraved on the surface.

"You satisfied, Sammy?" Duval asked.

"Sure am." His suspicions had been confirmed. There had been no confusion regarding burial sites. Madsen was not safely buried elsewhere at Lafayette Cemetery in the coffin Maire had supposedly purchased. Sam looked at the coffin number again. 585911. Right serial number, right casket, wrong body.

Sam recalled the hand written number on the catalogue sheet he had seen. His gut told him the serial number of the dead airman's casket had also been recorded as belonging to Madsen Cassaise after her disappearance. It had been entered by hand, so the serial number had been recorded for 2 different deads, the airman's and hers. But two bodies were not in the same casket, that was for damn sure. The assignment of a coffin number was obviously a cover. And someone had gone to the trouble of placing a headstone as further proof that the girl had been buried. Sam was now sure Madsen had never even been there.

Chapter 18

Beatrice was hungry. She stood on her hind legs with her front paws on the kitchen counter while she checked out the evening's bill of fare. When Sam didn't move fast enough to suit her needs, Beatrice got down and dragged her bowl a bit closer to the counter.

Sam dropped the can opener into the sink. His hands felt thick and awkward, which he shrugged off as a byproduct of the insomnia he was still experiencing.

He still hadn't been able to locate Charlie Biscay, and he had a bad feeling in his gut. On the way home from the mortuary, he had stopped by the floral shop Charlie owned and was surprised to discover that a guy named Craig now managing the business. When Sam asked Craig to relay a message, he said Charlie was no longer around.

"Doesn't Charlie Biscay still own the shop?" Sam asked.

"No, he sold it to my boss over a year ago. 'Needed the money for medical expenses. The new owner let him stay on to help out a few days a week and earn a salary, but he hasn't been in to work for two months."

"I wonder why Charlie didn't tell me," Sam said quietly.

"He probably didn't want anyone to feel sorry for him."

Now as Sam stood in the kitchen mentally re-playing the conversation, he felt like shit for not figuring it out sooner. He needed to find Charlie.

Beatrice now had one paw on the counter and one on his arm. She was sitting so close to his heels that he knew better than to step backwards. Her tail thumped up and down on the floor as he spooned food into her bowl. " 'She gets too hungry for dinner at eight,' " he sang as he grinned at the tooth impressions on her dish.

Suddenly the thumping stopped. When he looked behind him, his dog was gone. Sam stood perfectly still. She never walked away when she was about to be fed. "Beatrice?" he called.

Sam listened for movement. When he heard Beatrice's tail thumping again in the living room, his instincts went into full alert. Beatrice was not alone. Sam quietly slid the kitchen drawer open and pulled out his weapon.

When he inched toward the door to the living room, he caught Beatrice's reflection in the side window. She was chewing something, periodically thumping her tail as she ate. Sam could see that the screen door was closed and the lock appeared to be secure. It was then that his keen sense of smell took over.

Sam instantly burst into the room and rolled for cover behind an old sofa he had brought down from the attic. Sam took another deep whiff and then peered around the sofa. From his vantage point, he could now see Beatrice devouring a large beef bone. And the screen on the door had been ripped from its frame at the bottom.

Sam rolled again. In one move, he yanked the bone from Beatrice's mouth and continued rolling until he was pressed against the wall alongside the front door. When he heard movement, he peered out into the dusk and steadied his weapon. "I'm armed. Step onto the porch and show me your hands!"

A shadow moved into view. "Show me your goddamn hands!" Sam yelled again.

A blond woman suddenly stepped onto the porch frantically waving her hands. Sam stared in confusion. He knew the face, but something was amiss. The woman dropped one hand to her head then yanked off the blond wig revealing long dark hair.

"Sam, it's me," she said. "Ramona Slocum. From the Gentlemen's Club."

"Ramona!" Sam sighed with relief as he lowered his weapon.

"I received your message. That Bowser friend of yours from Los Angeles located my sister in Slidell and said I was to contact you."

"Where have you been?"

"Here and there. I got the message when I called her to see if anyone had been sniffin' around after me. I was relieved it was only you."

"Why didn't you knock?" he asked as he held the door open for her to enter. Ramona had to step around Beatrice, who was holding one paw in begging position in hopes of getting her bone back.

"I was here earlier and no one was home. I just assumed you were still gone 'cause I didn't see your car out front."

"It's in the barn."

"Oh. I'm sorry about the screen door. It's my fault, and I'd be happy to pay to fix it. When I first dropped by, Beatrice tried to climb through the screen after the bone. This time I slipped it through so she wouldn't do any more damage."

"No worries–the screen was already loose. And that explains why she didn't bark. She remembered you."

Ramona grinned. "Why did you take her bone away, Sam?"

"Big city cynicism. I was afraid someone threw her a poison bone to keep her still. It's an old trick burglars use."

Ramona looked around at the sparse furnishings skeptically.

"With all respect and stuff, what would a burglar want here?"

Sam laughed out loud. "Good question. I doubt anyone is after my good silver. But someone *has* taken a crack at my skull. How'd you find me?"

"I remembered you said you were staying at the family house in Chalmette, so I called back that Joe Bowser guy at L.A.P.D. and asked him the address."

"Good thinking. What's with the wig?"

"I don't want anyone to know I'm still in town, even though I'll be splitting soon."

He led her to the couch and gestured for her to sit. "Why are you leaving?"

"I got scared, Sam. Someone's following me. With Madsen disappearing like she did, I started to get all worked up."

"Did you tell the police someone was tailing you?"

"I told Duval, but he said there wasn't much they could do if I had no description or car or nothing."

"I see. So how do you know you're being followed?"

"I just know. But every time I look around the guy is gone. And one night a car pulled up alongside me real slow over on Toulouse. The car door opened, but the car took off real fast when some people stepped into view."

Sam was surprised at how young and vulnerable Ramona looked as she sank further down into the old brown sofa. "Did you see the car?" he asked as he moved to the window to check for any signs that Ramona had been followed.

"I just saw that it was big and dark."

"Two door?"

"Four. One person was driving, but someone in the back opened the door like they were gonna grab me. 'You think I'm paranoid?"

"Not at all. Did you-" Sam abruptly stopped talking when he heard the phone ring. He indicated for her to follow him into the bedroom as he went to answer.

"Lerner," Sam announced into the phone while gesturing for Ramona to sit at his desk. "Good work, Antoine," he said as he listened carefully.

Sam had called Tujagues Restaurant to ask Antoine to do some digging, and apparently his old friend had come up with some information. According to Antoine, although Charlie Biscay's rent had been paid through the end of the month, Charlie had indeed moved out. Antoine had one last tidbit of information before he hung up. "Charlie wasn't paying his own rent for a long time. It seems a friend had taken over the payments."

"Who else would be paying Charlie Biscay's rent?"

"Leon Duval. Were those two a couple?"

Sam could not even begin to formulate an answer.

* * *

"Charlie Biscay was a customer at the club," Ramona said after Sam hung up with Antoine. "I overheard you."

"Wrong Charlie. Charlie Biscay is gay."

"I know."

Sam looked at Ramona then sat down. "I'm getting too old to sort through all this gender fluidity," he groaned.

Ramona pushed up her sleeves and smiled. Sam was surprised to see an oddly masculine veil of hair covering her arms, which gave the illusion of a dark sweater. "Not everyone comes for sex," she explained as she unconsciously tugged at the hair. "You don't."

"I'm odd."

"Yes, but you're nice. You're just a little shy around women." Ramona laughed when Sam blushed. "Besides, we all know you dig Maire."

Sam smiled and looked away. It was true, he had been thinking about Maire a lot recently. But he felt guilty, like he was somehow blaspheming the memory of Kira. "Maire and I go back a long way," he nodded. "But back to Charlie please. Who did he see at the club?"

"Just Madsen. He used to tag along with Captain Duval. Charlie seemed like a lonely guy who just wanted a few laughs and some companionship. I know he liked Madsen a lot because she didn't seem to mind that he was sick."

"And Charlie never visited anyone else there?"

"No. Celeste tried to butter him up because she thought he had money, but she's too pushy for Charlie. He just wanted to hang out with a nice girl. It's nice to have an escort and go to some respectable places."

"Ramona, remember when you said there was a man who wanted to get Madsen out of there? Could that man have been Charlie Biscay?"

"Gee, I dunno. They certainly were close friends."

"Do you remember when Charlie last saw her?"

"Um, just before she disappeared, I think."

Sam shook his head. "I don't like any of this. I'm glad you're getting out of town, Ramona."

"Well, I can't leave until I get a place situated in Atlanta so I can work. That's where I'm headed."

"Then you can sleep on my couch for a few days where I can keep an eye on you."

"Thanks, Sam, I was hopin' you'd say that. So how come your hands are shaking?" she asked as she chased her shifting thoughts. "You need a drink?"

Sam, thrown completely off-guard by the blunt question, shoved his hands in his pockets. "I'm just tired," he mumbled. He had only gone to a few meetings, and his white-knuckle approach to achieving sobriety was not proving to be easy. That and lack of sleep were a killer combo.

"Looks like jumpy nerves to me," she insisted. "I guess you had a lot of harsh personal experiences back in L.A., huh?"

"Everything about Los Angeles is a harsh personal experience, Ramona," he muttered.

"No, I mean being a cop and all. It's kinda brutal. Don't L.A. cops beat up a lot of people?"

"No, we're a bunch of pussycats," he smirked.

"I guess cops have to stick together like a big family, huh? Like you and Captain Duval. I heard him tell Maire how much he depends on you."

"Ah, shit," Sam moaned. Duval had always placed Sam on a pedestal, and that's what pissed Sam off. He didn't need the guilt, and he didn't want to have to live up to anybody else's expectations.

"Yeah, Duval and I have a past, Ramona. But if you don't mind, I'd like to talk about something else. I need to figure out why Charlie Biscay lied to me about knowing Madsen." He reached for the mud-stained note he had found at Madsen's grave.

"That is odd. I could tell he felt close to her."

"Do you know who Madsen went to see in Belle Amie?" Sam inquired as he recalled the bus ticket stub in Madsen's drawer.

"Nope, she didn't say. But it was *past* Belle Amie. Some place out on the bayou, I think. Someone picked her up at the bus station."

Sam recalled passing through Belle Amie himself one Thanksgiving when he had gone to visit Charlie Biscay at Charlie's family's plantation home on Bayou Lafourche.

Sam wondered if his old friend had some reason to kill Madsen. Sam knew in his gut it was Charlie who had left the note at what was supposed to be Madsen's grave. And what in the hell was going on between Charlie and Leon Duval? He had to find Charlie Biscay to get some answers.

Chapter 19

Obscured by the shadow of a bent tree, Sam checked out the old plantation home for any signs of life. As the ancient oaks and cypresses drooped in their effort to hold up the layer of sweltering heat bearing down on the bayou, Sam remained still.

After several minutes of rest, he peeled his wet shirt away from his back and brushed the sweat from his forehead. His appreciation of air conditioning had shot up to an all-time high while walking the last mile to the Biscay family home.

By the looks of things, the plantation was as run down as Charlie had been the last time they spoke. And the old homestead displayed the same pallid hue as his friend. Sam knew Charlie had come home to die.

When slowly approaching the veranda, Sam was struck by the sad image of a house so parched it could barely anchor itself against the waves of heat rising from the front lawn. Still, the home's drooping roof seemed to bow to an elegant era long past–an era of music, parties, and opulent Southern hospitality. Two large oaks guarded the walk, their resurrection fern parasites offering a verdant and desperate dash of color to the tired façade.

Sam knew that most of Charlie's family had moved away or died off. He had tried calling, but the phones had long ago been disconnected, as had Charlie's mobile phone number. A cursory look would indicate the place was abandoned. However, trodden leaves and a pattern in the dust around the front door suggested that someone had recently used the entrance.

Sam raised his fist and knocked on the glass. After several fruitless attempts to get a response, he made his way to the back of the main house, peering through each dust-coated window he passed. The side service entrance was locked tightly, but the pile of dirt swept aside near the door in the back indicated that the rear entrance had also been used recently.

At the foot of the back stoop, a garbage bin hosted a swarm of flies who were scavenging for their mid-day meal. The hot metal seared Sam's hand when he removed the lid from the pail and hurled it to the ground. He silently cursed himself for being an idiot as the resounding crash rippled across the hollow porch. He paused to listen, but no one came.

At the bottom of the garbage can were several food wrappers and a partially eaten container of yogurt. After he waved away the persistent flies, he retrieved the carton. The expiration date on the bottom of the yogurt was an indication that Charlie, or someone, had been there very recently.

Sam held his breath as he fished to the bottom of the barrel to retrieve several plastic utensils. He inspected each carefully for signs of lipstick or anything else that might lead him to Madsen, if she had even been there. When his hand slid over a pile of maggots, he got pissed off all over again.

After he wiped his hand on the ground, Sam scanned the back of the house. At one end of the porch, pieces of vine clung like gnarled fingers to a thick wood trellis. Using the structure as a ladder, Sam hoisted himself up onto the porch roof before making his way along the second story wall.

He remembered from his visit long ago that Charlie's room was located at the back corner of the house. From his rooftop position, Sam peered in the window and waited for his eyes to adjust to the various shades of gray. He was able to distinguish a dresser, an old silk-covered divan, and a mahogany table.

The table was littered with dead plants, each a mass of brown decay. And, buried in the remains of each plant, was a jarringly bright yellow canary. One stuffed canary lay on its side on the table as if overcome by heat and starvation.

Next to the table was a four poster bed. Sam was startled when his eyes finally zeroed in on their pale target. Charlie Biscay lay in a heap on the rumpled bed gazing back at Sam with vacant eyes. Charlie's face, crumpled like a discarded shirt, was as lifeless as the canaries.

Sam knocked on the glass several times, but Charlie did not respond. Unable to budge the tightly sealed window, Sam took off his shoe, covered his eyes, and smashed the shoe against the glass. When the glass gave way, he was instantly repelled by the putrid odor of body waste and gangrene. He released the lock, shoved the window open, and crawled through.

"Charlie, it's me, Sam! Can you hear me?"

Charlie blinked as Sam approached the bed. He stared for a moment before nodding in recognition.

"I'm taking you to a hospital, buddy."

"No."

"You need help."

Charlie smiled weakly. "No hospital. The nurses will steal my tiara."

"Then we'll glue the damn thing to your head." As Sam bent over his old friend, Charlie lifted one claw-like hand in protest. "I'll cover the cost, Charlie. You need a doctor."

When Sam pulled the sheet aside, the odor was so overpowering he had to fight his gag reflexes. He slipped one arm under Charlie's light frame to lift him, but when he pulled the dying man upward, a mass of gangrenous tissue separated from Charlie's back, clinging to the sheets in a fleshy pulp. Charlie moaned in pain.

"I'll get a doctor out here," Sam promised. He gently lowered his friend back down on the bed and covered his frail body. The accumulation of liquid inside Charlie's lungs rattled his chest with each hacking cough. "For chrissake, buddy, you can't stay here. Not like this! Please let me help you."

Charlie stared at the wall and scowled. He said something indecipherable and then pointed to a stain on the faded silk wallpaper. "Kick that bastard's ass, Sam," he ordered.

Sam glanced at the wall, then back at Charlie. His friend was falling in and out of dementia. When Charlie, who was visibly agitated, once again scowled at the stain, Sam shook his fist at the imaginary enemy. "It's okay, I kicked his ass."

"Much obliged." Charlie took several breaths before he was able to speak again. "Barbra died," he cringed. "That ol' cat just keeled over on my balcony the day I was moving. I knew that was my cue to take my final bow, too."

Sam closed his eyes and shook his head, not knowing what to say. As he sat in silence, he stared at his old friend. Each time Charlie tried to speak, his face contorted with pain. Sam could smell death on his breath, a familiar odor he had smelled too many times in his life.

A croak suddenly escaped Charlie's throat. Sam was alarmed until it became evident that Charlie was laughing. "That dang canary looks better than I do. And he committed suicide. Damn ingrate didn't even leave us a note."

Sam smiled sadly. "Speaking of notes, I found your card at Madsen's grave."

"Ah, the scandal."

"You want to tell me about it?"

"No."

Sam sighed and turned away in frustration as he tried to gauge how far to push his terminally ill friend. He fumbled with a powder compact that was on the bedside table and then absently tugged at the dry leaves on a dead begonia. He stopped abruptly when he noticed the flower pot was set atop a thick piece of photo paper. With one finger, Sam slipped the photo out from under the pot.

Sam found himself staring down at a snap shot of Madsen, who was smiling sweetly back at him. She was wearing a black dress, and her silver locket was hanging protectively against her chest.

"Pretty photo," Charlie managed to say. "You can have it. But keep your mitts off my make-up."

"You goofy old pervert." Sam tried not to stare at Charlie, whose grin was stretched so tightly across his bones it reminded him of a burned carcass. Sam returned his focus to the leaves of the dead plant.

"You gonna stick around, Sam?" Charlie rasped. "Maire needs you."

"You may be right."

"And I suspect you're mighty lonely."

"What makes you think so?"

Charlie stared at the ceiling and pointed. When Sam looked up, he saw nothing. He suspected Charlie was hallucinating until Charlie opened his mouth to speak. After several failed attempts, Charlie found his voice again. "If you aren't lonely, why do you spend time with a faggot like me?"

"You're my friend."

"Bullshit, you just want my taffeta dress!"

Sam laughed and patted Charlie's hand. When Charlie closed his eyes, spittle oozed from one corner of his mouth. Sam gently shook him but could not elicit a response, so he shook him harder until Charlie finally opened one eye.

"Time for me to exit," Charlie whispered.

"Wait, buddy, don't leave yet. Please help me. I need to find out what happened to Madsen. You left a card at her grave."

A moan escaped from so low in Charlie's chest, it seemed as though he had taken his last breath. As Sam was reaching out to feel for a pulse, Charlie moaned again. "I should have helped her. I deserve to suffer." Sam was struck by the raw aching in his friend's voice.

"Why? Did you have a part in her disappearance?"

Charlie sunk further into the pillows in defeat, settling like a dry leaf.

"Tell me before you leave," Sam pressed. "Give me something I can tell her mother."

"My disease didn't scare Madsen. She said I was beautiful."

Sam stared at Charlie's corpse-like face with its gaping slash of grin. "You are," he said quietly.

"I loved her." Charlie's breathing became more labored, weakening rapidly with every effort to speak. "She took care of me, so I gave her flowers, and those little canaries she loved, and I put away some money for her."

"But you're broke-"

Charlie leaned into Sam again and clutched his arm. "No, there's money here in the property, and I wanted her to have it."

"That's very generous."

"But I let her down. That night I went to warn her. The guy she met–she knew him. He was bad, but I was too scared to stop them from leaving."

"Who was the guy?"

Charlie struggled to pull his lips away from his teeth, exposing a coat of thick white matter on his tongue. His dry skin sucked up the tears now trailing down his face.

"Who did she leave with, Charlie?" Sam repeated.

"Louis-" A cough rattled through his chest like metal balls on glass. Each time his body lurched upward, the smell of decay filled the room.

"Louis who?" Sam leaned closer to Charlie's lips as the light in his friend's eyes was dimming.

"Cat," Charlie whispered.

"Louis Cat?"

"No. See Cat," he repeated.

"You see a cat? I don't know what that means, Charlie! Charlie?"

"Heaven," Charlie said to the ceiling just as death finally claimed his emaciated body. His grimace slowly relaxed into a weary smile.

"Yes, Heaven. Have a great trip to Heaven," Sam whispered as the energy lifted from the dead man like waves of heat.

After several moments, Sam closed his friend's eyes. He tucked the photo of Madsen into Charlie's lifeless hand and whispered good-bye before crawling out onto the roof in the same manner in which he had entered.

Despite the searing heat of the asphalt tiles, he sat motionless on the rooftop, too depleted to move. Sad and frustrated, he mulled over Charlie's last words. Suddenly Sam bolted upright as the new and old information came together in his mind with complete clarity. He had figured out what Charlie was trying to tell him.

* * *

Sam stood at an ancient pay phone near the old Bayou Market where he had left his car. He could not get a signal on his cell phone, and the market phone was "all jacked up," according to the toothless proprietor at the counter. The weathered building appeared to be slumped under a cloak of death, a characteristic Sam was struggling in vain to outrun. Everything around him appeared as colorless as Charlie Biscay.

The sun, which had dropped low in the sky, was now creating shadows that crawled across the swamp area like alligators searching for prey. Two egrets, undaunted by his presence, eyed him curiously then continued to forage for food in the thicket near the marsh.

Sam pumped coins into the phone, hoping it still worked, while the bored store owner stood in the doorway, making no attempt to hide the fact that he was eavesdropping. Sam came to attention when someone yelled hello on the other end of the phone line.

"Duffault, it's Sam. Can you put Jem on the phone?"

When Sam got no response, he was about to hang up and try again until he heard the honey-smooth tone of Jem's voice.

"Sammy?"

"Jemima! How's my best girl?"

"I was sleeping, you rascal. Seems like that's all I do."

"Yes, you were napping when I dropped by yesterday. Did you get the little bottle of bourbon I left you?"

"What bottle?"

"Well, I-" Sam heard a low chuckle on the other end of the line. "Ah, you go easy on that, ol' girl," he laughed.

"Have you been okay, Sammy?"

"Sure, I'm okay." He didn't know if he was lying or telling the truth. "Why do you ask?"

"I had a vision. You need to carry your weapon, boy."

"I don't have a license here."

"Screw that. And don't argue with yo' mammy," she croaked. "Did you find that girl you were looking for? Madsen is it?"

Sam smiled. "Your memory will linger on long after you do, my dear. No, I haven't found her. Is she still alive, you think?"

"I'm not sure, but keep looking. She called out, and I saw her in a dark place where there's bad business. Have you learned to believe in my visions?"

"Well, I still ask when I need help, don't I?"

"Not often enough. You need to get out of your hard head and into your gut." Her low chuckle made him smile.

"We both do the same thing in different ways, Jem. Listen, I have something else you can help me with. Didn't you once hang out at a place named Cat's Heaven, or something like that? It was some backwater bar on the river, I think."

"Cat's Blues Heaven. Blues that these old feet could dance to till the morning came a-sneakin round. We used to-"

"Please deposit fifty cents," a recorded voice said, drowning out Jem's last words.

"Jem," Sam shouted into the phone, "I'm out of change. Where is Cat's Blues Heaven?"

"Outside St. Rose. Follow the old River Road west through Destrehan. It's hidden among the cypresses, but if you wait till dark, you can follow the music."

"Please call Maire at the club and tell her to meet me there," he yelled. Sam didn't have time to think about why. He just knew he needed Maire with him right now.

Sam clicked off as the recorded voice repeatedly asked for more money. He was short on change, short on patience; and he had the nagging feeling he was short on time.

Sam then rushed to the Shelby and hopped in. He would call 911 for Charlie once he could get a cell signal, but right now he was determined to find out where Madsen had spent that evening with Charlie. And who she had left with.

Before backing out, Sam checked his rear view mirror and was surprised to catch glimpse of a New Orleans police car coming up the road. Odd, Sam thought. The cop was a far stretch from his jurisdiction. And he was heading in the direction of Charlie's place. Either the cop's sense of direction stank, or something else did.

Sam pulled behind a dumpster and crouched low in his seat until the police car passed. When the vehicle was out of view, he turned the Shelby in the opposite direction and headed out onto the road. "Duval, are you just a jerk-off," he wondered, "or have you become something far more dangerous, ol' pal?"

Chapter 20

Celeste sat stiffly on the edge of a chair. She pressed her knees together and gazed at the image staring back at her from the vanity mirror. Her blond hair was tangled, but her scalp hurt too much to use a hair brush. The stained yellow flowers on the floral Victorian paper in the background accentuated the bruises that oozed beneath her skin like puddles, spreading slowly with each passing hour.

When she removed the top from a tube of Lidocaine and gingerly spread the ointment over her wrists, she winced, but she remained silent as the ointment bit into the rope abrasions. There was no way she would let the bastard witness her pain. That would be just one more way he controlled her, and Celeste wasn't about to give in to any man. Especially to Louis Santos.

Louis lit two cigarettes, got up off the bed, and walked over to the vanity. He held one cigarette under her eye almost close enough to burn her. When Celeste didn't flinch, he grinned and placed the cigarette between her dry lips. She inhaled deeply, the smoke curling from her nostrils up her face, as if trying to camouflage the welts in smears of gray. Louis placed his thick hands on her shoulders to massage her muscles. "You were great, baby," he said, allowing a stream of cigarette smoke to escape between his teeth.

"Yeah, so were you, you fucking pervert!"

Louis laughed heartily. "Don't play like you didn't like it. You're a whore. You ain't supposed to necessarily get off you know."

Celeste poured some whiskey over ice and sipped slowly. "You promised no more rough stuff. Do you think my other clients will want to make it with a woman who has a face like a prize fighter?"

Louis laughed again, however, this time the laugh was tainted with menace. "That's not my problem, you cunt. We have an arrangement, so shut the fuck up."

"The arrangement was that I keep you informed about the comings and goings of the girls you're hot for, and I keep quiet about what I know. And for my services, you pay me money. Lots of money. When did I say you could beat the crap outta me?"

Louis stopped rubbing Celeste's shoulders and stood very still behind her, his strong hands circling her neck. "Listen up, bitch," he said ominously, "I don't have to pay you shit. If you talk, you die."

"Then you'll go down with me."

In one move, he slid his hands around her neck. "I don't have to wait for you to shoot off your big mouth to get rid of you, you stinking tramp."

Celeste took another drag off her cigarette before placing it in a tin ashtray on the vanity. She jerked free from his grip and then turned to blow the smoke in his face. "No, you don't have to take that chance. But you will."

Louis grabbed her face and dug his thick fingers deep into her cheeks. He continued to squeeze the sides of her mouth while holding her fast.

After Celeste stared her tormentor down for a brief moment, she spoke again through puckered lips. "I fe-ew wike a weely big wabbit," she said, skillfully diffusing the tension of the moment. Louis let out a burst of laughter as he released his grip.

After Celeste rubbed her cheeks, she slid her fingers into her whiskey glass and pulled out an ice cube. She rubbed the ice along her battered face while Louis flopped back down on the bed.

" 'I fe-ew wike a wabbit,' " Louis repeated, holding his own cheeks. "That was pretty good. You crack me up, doll."

"Yeah, I'm pretty damn lovable."

"Yeah, right."

"You know you love me, Louis. And you need me because I'm your ticket into the Gentlemen's Club, which enables you to choose your 'sales inventory' as needed."

"You can be replaced."

"Don't kid yourself. None of the other girls will come near you. They heard about your crazy sex games and voodoo bullshit. Nowadays Maire lets you see only me 'cause she heard you're a psycho."

"Shut your fucking mouth!" Louis screamed jumping to his feet. He grabbed an ash tray off the bedside table and hurled it across the room. Celeste ducked just before it connected with the mirror, shattering the glass into an intricate web of broken pieces.

"I've told you not to call me that," Louis yelled as he rushed toward her. When he rounded the bed, he tripped over the strewn covers and let out a stream of profanity.

Celeste bolted closer to the door. "Okay, okay, baby. Easy now," Celeste soothed as she backed against the wall. "All I meant was that the other girls don't appreciate a real man."

Louis laid into her, pinning her against the wall. She grabbed for the door knob as he lifted her up off the floor. "Don't think I can't get another girl to set me up," he snarled.

"The only one you wanted is gone. Madsen is dead, Louis. And she was your mark, not a partner. So who you gonna call, 'Whorebusters'?"

"Who says I can't get the classiest broad of all?"

"Maire?" Celeste laughed bitterly. "She doesn't do the customers. She thinks of herself as an entrepreneur who's above it all. Besides, she can't stand you. Haven't you noticed that she won't speak to you or even look at you when you're around?"

"You're full of shit! There's a lot you don't know."

"I know you make her skin crawl."

"Stop saying that!" Louis screamed in her face. He pressed his squat body so hard against her she had to fight for breath.

Celeste knew she had pushed him far enough. She'd get back at him, but not now. He'd been drinking too much and he was too amped on coke. But she'd get him *after* she got her money out of the deal. "Sure. Sure, Louis," she gasped. "I just get jealous is all. You know I love you."

Louis slowly set Celeste back on her feet. He stared at her as if contemplating his next move, and then he pushed her hair back and gently kissed each bruise one at a time. "Don't be afraid, baby," he whispered, his hot breath coating her skin. "I love ya.' We've had some fun times since the good old days in Baton Rouge, eh?"

"Yeah, fun times. Let's go back to bed, sweetie. Then you can take me shopping at some really fancy stores like you promised," she bartered.

Louis grinned, bowed, and then bolted for the bed. He jumped on the mattress and bounced up and down like a school boy. After a few minutes of play, he reached for the nipple clamps.

Celeste slipped off her robe. She reminded herself that she was being paid big bucks to keep quiet, so she would do whatever she had to do to get the money she needed to leave all this shit behind forever. Surely an occasional romp in the sack with the sick prick couldn't hurt her. Or so she thought.

Chapter 21

Sam pulled off of the old river road outside of St. Rose and switched on the overhead light. *Gotta get me a GPS*, he reminded himself. Even above the engine, he could hear the crickets calling back and forth to each other along the river bank. After Sam checked his map, he rolled the window down further. Jem was right. Distant blues notes throbbed through the heavy air above the trees confirming that he was on the correct road to Cat's Blues Heaven.

When he leaned over to roll down the passenger window, he noticed headlights in his rear view mirror. A classic 1967 Mercedes 250SL pulled up alongside him and flashed its lights.

"You must be horny as hell to have me drive all the way out here to meet you, Sam Lerner," a female voice called out into the night. "Fortunately, 'Serving Others' is my motto."

Sam laughed. "And I'm sure no one does it better, Maire."

"You want to find out?"

"You'd kill me. But thanks for coming. The place we're going to is straight ahead," he gestured.

"As long as it's not a Klan meeting, lead the way, chere."

They turned onto a dirt road and traveled another two hundred yards to a tin-covered road stop nestled into the river bank. After parking their cars behind a shroud of Spanish moss, they got out and followed a row of Japanese lanterns that led them under an oak canopy to the open front door. The contrast was remarkable. Strings of colored lights lined the roof of the establishment, which was spilling over with music and revelers. Several people nodded and tipped their hats as they entered.

The interior of the bar was lined with rough wood. Neon lights advertising various libations saturated the walls with color, and a ceiling canvas was pulled back to expose the room to the balmy night. When Sam glanced up, he saw stars so large they seem perched to drop in through the open rafters.

"I feel out of place here," Sam said to Maire above the saxophone soloist.

"Because we're not black?"

"Hell, no–'cause I'm not wearing a hat!"

Sam enjoyed Maire's low-pitched laugh. His eyes had already sized up her short, figure-hugging dress and matching sling-back heels. Sam let out a low whistle as he checked out her long legs clad in black stockings. "Gee I'm glad those things are back in fashion."

"Legs?"

Sam laughed and shook his head as he pulled out a chair for her at a small bistro table near the back of the dance floor. "Legs like that never go out of style. I mean those striped stockings."

"Fishnet," she laughed, "and they're my own style." She looked around and smiled. "So this is Cat's Blues Heaven. This place is a legend among the locals."

"So how have we missed it all these years?"

"It hasn't been integrated all that long. We're in the South, remember?"

A black woman in a flowered dress suddenly slid a plate of ribs in front of them. "Appetizers. They're on the house for newcomers. We ain't never seen you two here before, have we?"

Sam stood up and shook her hand. "We'd never admit it anyway, not with free ribs like that at stake. I'm Sam, and this is Maire. Thanks for the hospitality."

"Servin' up a plate of ribs kinda beats throwing tomatoes as a welcome, don't it? I'm Carolina, *Mrs.* Kool Cat to those who might have a rovin' eye for my man." Carolina's hearty laugh exploded through a set of perfect teeth as she nodded toward a wiry man who was polishing the old wooden bar with a towel.

"I think you know the Creole woman who raised me," Sam told her. "She used to come here a lot when she was younger. Her name's Jemima."

"Jemima?"

Sam felt himself flush with color. "Well, I called her that when I was a young boy," he stammered. "I didn't know it might be offensive and I-"

Carolina stopped him with a loud guffaw. "Whatcha drinking, hon? Never mind. I'm gonna send you something special." Carolina walked off before he could protest.

Sam glanced at Maire's bemused expression. "I think I just made an ass of myself," he muttered.

She smiled then leaned in close enough for him to smell her warm skin. "But you do it so humbly."

Within minutes Carolina returned and slapped down three iced mugs of dark brew. "Cat's special," she announced. "He calls it Ape Piss 'cause it'll put hair on your back and make you swing from the drapes. Let's drink to Jem. I love that old gal."

Sam hesitated as Carolina furled a brow and waited. Finally he grabbed the mug and took a small sip to avoid any further offense to Carolina. He could feel the alcohol as it went down, slowly smoothing the sharp edges inside him. He couldn't remember when he had felt so warm and so cool at the same time. He raised his glass as a toast then drank again.

Carolina wiped her mouth with the back of her hand. "It's whiskey, ale, and lime, with a dash of Cat's secret spice. He'll be over later to check your pulse. So how's that mammy of yours? She was here only a month ago."

"Jem? You must be mistaken. She's too old to get around much."

"No mistake," Carolina protested holding up one large, walnut colored hand. "It was Jemima all right. She once told me her 'son' named her that. Anyway, she got a cab to bring her all the way out here from town."

Although Sam smiled to hear that Jem had referred to him as her son, he wasn't sure why he was proud and sad at the same time. "A cab, huh?" was all he managed to say.

"Yep, that ol' girl has so much spirit you'll have to nail her in the coffin when her time comes. And I think she knows her time is coming, son. She gets the visions."

"Yup," Sam nodded.

"I see you're a skeptic," Carolina observed, never losing her easy-going demeanor.

"Not completely, but I'm a cop. We deal in facts."

"Well, here's a fact for 'ya. Lotsa people in these parts believe she's got the gift. Jem used to read the shells and cards for our customers. She's royalty here. I think she came all the way out here because she wanted one last dance with Cat."

"She was dancing?" Sam looked at Carolina and Maire in amazement.

"In her fashion. Right up there in front of everyone. You'da been proud." Carolina finished off her drink and sauntered off, clapping enthusiastically as the saxophone player tipped his hat to the appreciative clientele.

After he watched her leave, Sam shook his head and gulped his drink. "I should have known Jem was still full of piss-and-vinegar. For an ex-detective, I sure as hell can't see what's in front of me."

Maire placed her hand on his. "If I drink this, I won't be able to see at all," she grinned as she pushed her drink toward him. "Drink mine. I don't want to offend her. Offense is your department."

"Thanks for the support," Sam smirked, deciding he could stop drinking again tomorrow. He finished off his drink then reached for hers, brushing his hand up her leg as he leaned in.

"Do you want to tell me why we're here?" she smiled.

"I wanted to see you, isn't that enough?"

Maire moved closer and brushed her lips against his cheek. "It always has been, chere. But I'm not sure it's enough anymore."

Sam felt his face flush. "Maire-"

"Don't say anything, Sam. We're older now, and we both need each other. We're running out of time."

Sam set down his mug and held her face in both hands. "We're not running anywhere. I do want to talk about this, babe. I think of you all the time. But right now I need to get a few urgent questions answered. We can wait a little longer, can't we? We're always going to be us. You and me."

Maire nodded her head as she settled into the crook of his arm. "Okay, I can wait. So for the last time, why are we here?"

"I think this is where Madsen came on the last night anyone saw her alive."

"Sam, leave this alone."

"Maire, she was with my old friend, Charlie Biscay. He came to your place with Leon Duval a few times. He died today."

"Yes, Jem told me. Of course I remember dear Charlie, and I'm so sorry. I know you were friends for a long time."

Her large green eyes were looking deeper inside him than he wanted anyone to see. The intimacy of her stare flustered Sam. He averted his gaze, resorting to his well-practiced emotional camouflage. "I'm just trying to piece things to-gether," he explained. "I saw Leon Duval on his way to Charlie's house within minutes of Charlie's death. That's damn coincidental."

Maire groaned. "Poor Leon. He'll be so upset. He's been trying to locate Charlie for several days. He picked up Charlie's medicine for him, but Charlie had dropped out of sight. Leon told me he planned to go out to Charlie's family estate to try to find him."

"Nice timing," Sam mumbled. "I could have sworn Duval was looking for me."

"That's pure paranoia. He's only looking *out* for you. In fact, he dropped by my place yesterday to see if you were there."

"Jesus Christ. It's like he has a hard-on for me!"

"Well, who could blame him? But he said he wanted to take you out to Domilise's for an oyster po-boy. He has always looked up to you, Sam. He's like a little kid when you're around, always seeking your attention and advice. That's why he asked you to talk to Madsen's mother."

"What choice did he have? It was fairly obvious I'd start asking questions once I heard about Madsen's disappearance."

"True, but you know he'd love to bring you aboard to work with him so you can be the team you were back at Tulane."

"Those days are long over."

"Yes, maybe he lives in the past, but that's all he's got now that Linny left him for another man. Give the poor guy a break. Remember who your friends are, love."

Maire was right, and now Sam felt like shit-on-a-shoe. Duval had always had his back and had followed him around like a St. Bernard, hoping for a chance to rescue him and prove his worth. "I guess my trust quotient is pretty low. Maybe living in L.A. has given me too many hard edges. I'll try to cut him some slack."

"Yes, just let him play the part of the hotshot quarterback for a change."

"Yes, ma'am. See how good I am about taking orders?"

Maire smiled and leaned in closer to him. "Let's not talk about Leon Duval anymore. I just got you back, and I don't want to share you with anyone."

By the time Sam finished Maire's drink, he felt so relaxed his body seemed weightless. He slid his hand out from under hers and placed it on top. Maire grinned as she turned to listen to the band. "I hope you don't always have to be on top," she said out of the corner of her mouth.

Sam chuckled. "You're teasing me, woman, and you shouldn't tease a starving man."

She gave him a seductive look then suddenly jumped up. "Come on, Sam, let's dance."

As Sam let Maire lead him to the dance floor, he was aware his legs felt like sponges. "Christ, babe, I can't dance when I'm *not* drinking, so how in the hell do you expect me to dance now?"

"Shhh, I've seen you move."

Sam stood in the middle of the crowd and breathed in the scent of sweat and cologne. Although the overhead fans were struggling to lift the heat from the floor, the temperature was even hotter near the band. Sam took Maire into his arms and began to waltz lazily around the old oak floor. As he swayed to the music, the room gradually became a blur of blues and reds, each face grainy from the smoke and the effects of the alcohol.

Sam focused on Maire. Her dress was clinging to her damp skin forming a V where her legs came together. He could see the outline of her pubic mound, and he felt himself growing hard. He was sure she noticed, but he was too dizzy to be embarrassed.

After several dances, they sat back down. Sam ordered another Ape Piss for himself and a glass of wine for Maire. This time Cat delivered the drinks himself. "Welcome to Cat's Blues Heaven." He set down the drinks and slapped Sam on the back in a hearty greeting. He gallantly kissed Maire's hand before turning back to Sam. "Carolina tells me you're Jem's boy, although with them blue eyes you got, I can't see no resemblance," he grinned playfully.

"Well, I'm practically kin. She raised me."

"I know. She brags about you whenever the wind blows. We heard you solved a lot of big cases up north. I got some family up there. They all know to call Sam Lerner if ever there's trouble."

Sam thought about what the old man was saying. Even strangers knew his name. And it was because of Jem. Sam knew that since Kira's death, he had not given Jem as much time and thought as she had given him. He had learned to distill his emotions into a palatable drink of isolation and denial, and now he regretted it. As Sam chugged his drink, he noticed how much easier each one went down.

"Good shit, eh?" Cat grinned. "So hows come you and this fine lady came all the way out to these parts? I'm sure it wasn't to dance with the brothers, 'cause I seen you dance."

Maire let out a low laugh as she got up to dance by herself. Sam felt a hint of breeze and leaned in its direction as he studied her seductive moves under the warm lights. In spite of his reluctance to tear his eyes away from the view, he pulled out a chair and gestured for Cat to sit down. "Several weeks back a girl came in here. She was light-skinned, biracial, early twenties, with long brown hair." He took out his wallet and flashed the photo of Madsen he had received from her mother.

After Cat studied the photo, he nodded and slid it back across the table. "This gal came in here with Charlie Biscay."

"So you knew Charlie?"

"What do you mean by 'knew'?"

"He's dead, Cat."

"Damn. He was a real nice guy, and one of our regular white folk. We don't get many, so you folks is easy to remember. Always over-tipping," he winked.

"That's the effects of the Ape Piss. No wonder you dole 'em out."

"I like your sense of humor, son. Charlie used to drop in whenever he traveled between his house and town."

Sam flashed the photo again. "Her name is Madsen. Do you remember if she was wearing the locket she has on in the photo?"

"Madsen, huh? Well, she was fiddlin' with some kinda necklace. That's how I could tell from across the room that she was nervous."

"Nervous?"

"Well, not with Charlie, but later. Her and Charlie were having fun, I could tell. Then she suddenly up and left with someone else."

"Do you know who?"

"I don't know the dude. Dark, stocky, and crude. He came in and sat down at their table like he knew them. I didn't catch his name when Charlie introduced him to me. When I asked him to repeat it, the guy just said to call him 'Saint,' like that was his nickname or something."

"And Madsen left with the guy?"

"Yep. Charlie tried to stop her when she stood up, but she asked him to sit back down. She looked scared, like she didn't dare say no to the other cat. The dude wasn't strong-armin' her though, so I had no call to get out my ball bat. That's all I heard. A few John Lee Hooker protégées had dropped in to jam, and the place was shakin' like tits on a stripper. I could tell Charlie was real upset, but he didn't dare say nothin' to the guy. He just sat with his head in his hands and watched 'em leave."

"Did he follow them?"

"Nope, 'just sat and drank. When I took him some eats, he mumbled something to me about trying to warn her, and then he got sick and ran outside. I never saw him again after that."

"Do you remember anything else about the guy Madsen left with?"

"Not much. I didn't see his car."

"Was he smoking a cigar?"

"Matter of fact, he was. And he was carrying a lot of bread. But you didn't hear it from me. I don't want no trouble."

"I've never even been here, Cat," Sam nodded. "And by the way, I've had a headache for three weeks, but it's finally gone." Sam lifted his drink in a salute before polishing off its remains.

"Wait till morning," Cat laughed, saluting him back.

When Sam looked up, he noticed Maire making her way back to the table. Most of the other male customers noticed, too.

Before Cat could relinquish her chair, Maire lowered herself onto Sam's lap. As she continued to move to the slow beat of the music, she pressed her damp body closer to his. Sam could feel his desire mounting. He tried to focus his attention on Cat, who was smirking at him like a coon hound.

"Boy it's hot in here," Cat grinned. "I think I'll get me a breath of night air." He chuckled and excused himself with a slight bow.

"Thanks, Cat," Sam called to his host. He brushed his cheek against the back of Maire's neck as he watched the older man exit.

Suddenly Sam sat upright and grew perfectly still. He squinted his eyes and peered beyond Cat out into the darkness. Half-hidden by the hanging cypresses that lined the old dirt road was the unmistakable shape of a police vehicle.

Sam slid Maire off his lap and struggled to rise to his feet. As he watched through an alcohol haze, the car's engine turned over. With its headlights off, the car pulled out slowly, then it disappeared into the night.

* * *

Sam felt a stirring he hadn't had since Kira died. It filled his chest and pressed against his groin. His mouth was dry, but his senses were magnified. His sense of smell was so intense he could almost taste Maire's skin as she leaned against him in the front seat of her car.

"Are you sure you're okay to drive?" she asked.

"Of course. You could wake up a mummy."

"Maybe I should drive you back to my place."

"I'll follow you, babe. I'm good. And I'd prefer not to leave my car here."

Slowly he leaned in to kiss her, surprised by how sweet she tasted. When he covered Maire's full lips with his own, it felt as if every nerve in his body was coming to life. He was shaking again, but this time for a different reason.

Maire's moans filled his mouth. When she pressed her breasts against his chest and draped her arms around his neck, Sam wanted to absorb her through his skin. "Let's get out of here," he whispered.

Sam waited for Maire to start her car before climbing into his. After fumbling with his seat belt, he managed to start the engine and turn on the headlights. He passed her Mercedes slowly and made sure he could see her in his rear view mirror before proceeding along the dirt road that ran parallel to the river.

Sam rolled his window down so he could breathe in the rich air of the Mississippi. It was a blend of fish, cypress and mud, a familiar scent he loved. He checked his watch: 2:35 A.M. No wonder he was craving scrambled eggs and fried green tomatoes with remoulade sauce. And Maire.

Sam knew of a little place he would take her later for a breakfast, but he had other things on his mind now. It felt good to want a woman again. It had been a very long time since he felt so alive.

Sam maneuvered the Shelby through the incoming fog with ease while he followed the road along the river bend. As he picked up speed on the straight-away along the bank, the rush of night air parted his damp hair like cool, soothing fingers.

The fog rolled over the windshield, creating shadows that were just beyond his front bumper. Sam slowed his car to make sure Maire was still following. When he spotted headlights behind him, he gave the car some gas and eased onto the gravel part of the old river road.

Sam immediately knew he was in trouble when the Shelby hit a slimy patch of road and started to fishtail. The mist and mud had made the road slippery, and his tires fought in vain to adhere to the crumbled road surface. As he turned his wheel in the opposite direction of the swerve, he spotted a car bearing down upon him, seemingly unable to keep track of his shimmying tail lights in the fog. The car had passed Maire's Mercedes and was going too fast for the condition of the old road. Sam gave his car some gas and tried to get out of the way.

When the Shelby suddenly slid to the right, its rear wheels sank into the ditch between the shoulder and the slope of the river bank. Sam could feel the car resist as he tried to bring it up out of the jagged rut alongside the road, which was carved deep from the heavy water run-off. He held tightly to the steering wheel and eased down on the brakes, but the speed of the car continued to propel the Shelby forward.

Suddenly Sam felt something slam into the rear driver's side of his car. He heard glass and saw lights as his car began what seemed like a slow motion spin. The front of the car lifted up, tilting him backward like a slow motion carnival ride. When the front dropped back down again, Sam had the vague notion he was rolling. After the spinning stopped, a heavy silence surrounded him.

Sam tasted grass and mud, but when he tried to reach up to clear his mouth, his arm wouldn't cooperate. The mist formed undulating ghosts that scuttled about him as he sought his bearings. His head felt damp, and a pain was crushing his temples and spreading backward toward his crown. In spite of his loss of equilibrium, he breathed deeply and tried to remain alert. As he exhaled, the acid in his stomach shot upwards burning everything in its path.

Sam could hear Maire's voice in the distance. He tried to ask her if she was okay, but he couldn't locate her. Then he heard another voice, but he couldn't make out the words.

The metallic taste in his mouth made him nauseous, and he was so cold he couldn't stop shaking. Gradually he rolled further onto his belly, seeking quiet and warmth. He groaned into the wet earth and closed his eyes.

Chapter 22

Renee Oleyant sat in the softly lit parlor and looked around at the voodoo symbols and offerings that filled the small Creole cottage. Heavy candle smoke lapped at an upside down cross on the cluttered altar and stopped to hover over several crude rattles that lay at the foot of the cross, ready to summon the deities. Drum rhythms were intense as the arms of smoke reached out to lift her from her chair.

The color-saturated house in the French Quarter was a welcome contrast to The Good Deal Inn where Renee had recently been staying. The Inn was washed with a gray pallor, a bland statement of noncommittal to anything alive that might pass through its metal, windowless doors.

Renee felt safe in the warmth of the cottage as she stared down at the small photo of her daughter. She had placed the snapshot of Madsen next to a bottle of rum, a packet of Marlboros, and the medicine pouches she had brought with her as offerings.

An old woman sat at the small table before her, her dark skin shining with sweat as she bent over the shells. Renee was mesmerized by the woman's long hands, which looked as if they were carved from walnut. The knuckles were stiff with arthritis, yet the woman managed to move quickly, silently, using only her knuckles to turn over the shells. Occasionally the woman would pause to stare at Renee or to sip some rum before falling back into her trance-like silence.

Renee Oleyant knew she had not been a good mother. She had become pregnant by a john when she was still a child herself. Perhaps she should have given Madsen up, but she had never had anything of her own. Blindly hoping that one day a man would allow her to leave the life by providing a home for her and her baby, she had sold herself to many men who offered false hope.

Renee Oleyant had aged quickly. Crack cocaine had eased the emptiness that would set in each morning while she counted what few bills some stranger had left on the battered Formica kitchen table. She had often turned a blind eye to her customers' nocturnal wanderings to the adjacent room in her ramshackle house. She would light the pipe and forget everything, including her child who was sleeping in that room.

Even though she was now clean, she knew she had lost her chance to make things right. She was glad Madsen had run away to save herself. But now her daughter needed help, and Renee was determined to make one last effort to save her. She believed it was the one redemptive act that could justify her own troubled journey on this earth. In Renee's own broken and unhealthy way, Madsen had been the only thing she had ever cared about. And Renee Oleyant was seeking forgiveness.

Renee had become increasingly distressed when she could not reach Sam Lerner about news of her daughter. She could no longer wait for help from the police she decided, and she was not going to be summarily dismissed. She wanted answers. And it had taken little effort to find the voodoo priestess who was known for her visions.

Renee watched as the old woman chewed the tip off a cigar and lit it. The priestess rubbed her eyes with her fingertips to try to push aside the cataract coating that sometimes dulled the visions. "I cannot see clearly tonight. And I do not wish to share bad news," the woman said quietly. "I am old, and I have seen too much. I sometimes get confused."

Renee's heartbeat quickened. "I was told you are the best," she whispered. "Do you need more money?"

"No, but I don't think we should continue this. I'm sorry."

As the woman reached to gather the shells, Renee placed her elegant hand flat atop the old woman's. The heat from the priestess's skin was more intense than anything Renee wished to feel at that moment. "Tell me, please," Renee commanded.

The woman hesitated and took a long drink from the bottle of rum before walking stiffly to the sofa. Slowly she sat down and stared out the window. "The girl is dead," she sighed. The remorse in her voice rendered her words almost inaudible. "Her struggle is finally over," she whispered.

Renee gasped. Her body refused to move as she watched the old priestess blow out the candles. Finally she stood, commanding her legs to carry her toward the door. "Thank you, Jemima," Renee said mechanically before making her way out into the noisy streets of the Vieux Carre.

Chapter 23

Sam blinked his eyes and touched his forehead. The pressure in his skull had awakened him from a deep dream in which he was drowning. The water had been up to his nose, slowly squeezing his temples. For a moment he was glad to be awake…until he felt the pain in his face. He winced and blinked several more times until he become aware that Maire was hovering over him.

"You're a mess alright," she smiled sympathetically.

When Sam looked around, he realized he was in Maire's suite of rooms on the third floor of the Gentlemen's Club. The familiarity of the carved wood fireplace and the lush Persian carpets gave him a sense comfort, in spite of the pain he felt from the waist up. "Ohhh," he moaned, "what did you do to me, woman?"

"It was your own doing, chere. We were leaving Cat's Blues Heaven, remember?"

"Oh, yeah. Are you okay?"

"I'm fine, and you'll be fine, but the Shelby is in intensive care."

"Now I really need a drink," he grunted. "How's your car, babe?" he asked as he tried to ignore her breasts, which were sneaking a peak at him through her sheer white blouse.

"I'm not the one who hit you, Sam. Somebody passed me, got between us, and was bearing down on you. I couldn't make out the car in the fog, but it seems you saw his headlights and swerved to avoid him. Your car slid off the shoulder and rolled down the bank. You hadn't fastened your seat belt properly, so you were thrown from the car into marsh. The other guy kept on going."

"So I'm still in one piece?" Sam asked, too tired to take inventory.

"I suppose, but you do have a lot of bruises and lacerations. Maire grabbed his hand as he reached for his face." Don't touch. I placed ice packs on your nose and head. You've been slightly renovated."

"Christ, soon I'm gonna need a building permit. So you drove me back here?"

"Yes. You refused to go to a hospital, and you groused about your car the entire time. I gave you some Vicodin, so you've been asleep awhile. I had the Shelby towed to Hank's Overhaul for repairs. The events of the evening will all come back to you once you eat a hot meal and the drugs wear off."

"What's that weight on my legs?" Sam tried to examine his lower half, but he couldn't sit up.

"Relax, Sam, you're not paralyzed if that's what worried about. It's Beatrice. I sent Celeste over to pick her up. She's been trying to lick your wounds to heal you."

"Celeste or Beatrice?"

"Both."

Sam laughed and reached down to stroke Beatrice's head. He then placed one hand on Maire's leg. "Thanks, babe. I hadn't planned to end up in your bed this way."

"Hell, it's the closest we've come in twenty-five years, chere. Wait until you've healed. Then we'll negotiate. I prefer that my men be conscious."

"At least until you're done with them," he retorted. Sam tried not to grin because his head hurt every time his face moved.

He was reaching for a bottle of aspirin on the bedside table when Celeste stepped into the room. Sam was shocked at her appearance. It was apparent that her blond hair was pulled down over her eyes to cover a mass of bruises.

"Here's the dog's bowl, Maire," Celeste said, keeping her face down. When she realized Sam was staring at her, she turned to leave. "I'm glad you're okay, Mr. Lerner," she said formally over one shoulder as she exited the room. He noticed that Celeste was limping.

"Jesus, Maire, what in the hell happened to Celeste?"

"Nice piece of work, huh? Some date did that to her. She won't talk, but I think she's got some sick relationship going on with someone she's known for a while. I've seen signs of it before."

"I thought you didn't allow that."

"It didn't happen here." Maire sighed and looked away. "It's her business what she does on her free time, Sam."

"Did she file a report?"

"No, she refused."

"Do you have any idea who the fucker is who did that to her?"

"I asked Leon Duval to check it out. Now be quiet while I get you some soup."

Sam gestured to Beatrice, who was now standing at the foot of the bed holding her bowl in her mouth. "Maire, I hate to be a pain in the ass, but has the dog eaten?"

"Uh-huh. Twice. Beatrice got beef brisket. You get the broth."

"I'd prefer some of your ass-kicking jambalaya with Andouille sausage and shrimp."

"Maybe later. Broth first."

When Sam let out a greatly exaggerated groan, Maire laughed and turned to go. As Sam watched her walk down the hall, he enjoyed the way her hips swayed, as though carrying on a conversation of their own. He smiled and leaned back into the pillow, happy to be cared for.

* * *

Celeste sat in the rocker in her room and stared out the window at the purple Morning Glories that scaled the courtyard walls. The dull ache in her bruised neck was a constant reminder not to swallow any more than necessary.

In the reflection of the window, her face was distorted, as if too large for her thin neck. Her dark roots needed a touch-up, but she didn't give a damn. Glancing down at her hands, she observed how the polish on her nails was chipped and peeling. The dark red lacquer was the color of blood. One day soon it will be his blood, she decided.

Shaking her head in disgust, she recalled how she had once cared about the sick freak. They had shared some good times when they were younger, but that was before his preferences became increasingly sadistic. Now the bastard deserved to die.

She and Louis had been playing a game of control that had reached a dangerous point. And she was losing. The psychopathic son-of-a-bitch was evil and crazy, but she needed her money. A deal was a deal, and she wasn't leaving town without getting what she was due. After all, she had earned it.

While continuing to stare at her own distorted image in the window, Celeste reached toward her bed, slipped her hand under her pillow, and felt for the steel object. It was still there.

It had been a fortuitous turn of events when Maire asked Celeste to drive out to Sam Lerner's place to pick up the dog and some clothes for Sam. It had allowed time for her to work out her plan more carefully.

While rifling through Sam's kitchen drawers, Celeste had come upon the easiest solution to her problem. She would indeed collect her money from Louis before leaving town; and directly after she got paid she would corner the bastard during a vulnerable moment when he wouldn't be able to defend himself. Then she would kill him.

She planned to leave him so fucking dead it would seem he had never, ever existed. Celeste smiled as she pictured it. Yes, she would kill him so dead he would even die in his next cruel, sick life. And Sam Lerner's gun would do the job quite well, thank you very much.

Chapter 24

Sam sat propped up in Maire's bed. One hand cradled his cell phone while the other hung over the side of the bed, holding a dog biscuit for Beatrice to munch on. As he waited on hold, he stared down at his growing file on Madsen, which had been retrieved for him from his place in Chalmette.

In spite of the fact that Ramona could trust Maire, Sam had called Antoine at Tujagues Restaurant and asked his old friend to drive out to warn Ramona that someone from the Gentleman's Club would be dropping by. Sam wanted to honor Ramona's request not to divulge her whereabouts, and he knew Ramona had lucked out once by not being there when Celeste had gone by. Two times would be tempting fate.

According to Antoine, all signs had indicated that Ramona had already moved on. Sam hoped she had gotten out of town fast so she wouldn't be followed again.

Sam pressed the phone closer to his ear when his friend at L.A.P.D. came back on the line. "His nickname is 'The Saint,'" Sam said into the phone. "Check anything that might be similar, Joe. This guy must have a record. Start with Baton Rouge connections. That's where the victim, Madsen Cassaise, had been residing before coming here. And don't go through anyone in the New Orleans Police Department. I don't know who's clean."

While Sam waited for Joe to answer another call, he stared at an article he had cut out of the *Times Picayune* and placed in Madsen's file right after she disappeared. He was staring at the print when Joe came back on the line.

"I thought you retired, buddy," Joe said into the other end of the phone. "Didn't you ride off into the sunset to be a night watchman or to fish with Furman and all our other renegade cops now living in Idaho?"

"Funny stuff, Joe. I *am* retired. I'm calling from bed, and it's the middle of the day."

"I hope you're not alone. Did you look up the lovely Maire you've told me so much about?"

Sam instinctively glanced out the long windows that lined one wall of the room. He could see Maire down in the garden clipping roses for a bouquet. Sam smiled as he watched her graceful movements. "I'm in the lady's bed right now," he drawled. "But don't jump to any conclusions."

Joe let out a rooster crow on the other end of the phone. "I'm coming down there the first vacation I get," Joe laughed.

"Well, can you do me another favor before you pack?"

"Sure thing. Whattya need?"

Sam scanned the newspaper article again and underlined a name. "See what you can dig up on the case of a girl who drowned here just before I arrived. Find a subtle way to get around local police. Her name was Carol Stone, as in stone cold dead."

"Got it."

"See if Coroner Malcolm Wilson signed her death certificate."

"Okay. Will you be there awhile?"

"Uh-huh, I'm hurtin' like a kicked dog."

"Jesus, she must be a helluva ride," Joe teased. "Try to stay in one piece. I'll buzz you right back."

After Sam hung up, he continued to stare at the newspaper article until it dawned on him what hunch had led him to save a copy of the story. Carol Stone had turned up dead just before Sam returned to New Orleans. She was a drowning victim like Madsen, close in age, no relatives, occupation unknown, origins unknown, and a prostitute. He had smelled a pattern. And he still did.

Sam stood up and steadied himself, pissed as how the effects of the Vicodin lingered like L.A. smog. He opened the window and yelled down to Maire, who was alone in the courtyard.

"Hey babe, did you ever have a girl here named Carol Stone?"

Maire shielded her eyes against the sun and looked up at him. "No, Sam."

"You're sure?"

"Yes, unless she was the one who stayed here briefly a few months back. The short-timers often use different names."

"Do you know where that girl went?"

"No, I have no idea."

Sam nodded then closed the window just as his cell phone rang again. "Joe?"

"Yeah, Sam. The official line is that Carol Stone, aka Cara Spencer, drowned and was sent to Potter's Field as an unclaimed body. Wilson signed the certificate. However, the cemetery I called couldn't find her in the records."

"What a surprise," Sam said sarcastically.

"I'll keep digging."

"Thanks. Later, buddy." Sam pulled on his pants, chugged down a glass of juice, and shoved his phone into his pocket. He had some digging of his own to do.

* * *

As Sam sat across the desk from Coroner Malcolm Wilson, he could smell the old man's rancid breath and strong perspiration. Sam had caught him by surprise when he forced his way into the office. Wilson was in no mood to talk, nor did he seem to be in any condition to talk. The coroner's face was even more yellow-orange than when they had first met, as if it had been dusted with flower pollen. And his syrupy eyes were lifeless.

Sam laid his weapon on the desk, a signal that he was not about to offer up any social pleasantries. "I know you're concealing evidence, Wilson. So I think it's time we have a little come-to-Jesus moment here today."

"I don't have to talk to you, Mr. Lerner. I'm having you removed from this office."

"If you're being paid to keep silent, no amount of cash will save your ass in a federal penitentiary." Sam shoved a newspaper under the coroner's face before he could pick up the phone. "Carol Stone drowned shortly before Madsen Cassaise did, and she was sent to Potter's Field, but they have no record of her there. Madsen's body is missing, too. There are too many similarities."

"I don't know what you're getting at."

"Sure you do. And when I prove that the disappearance of these girls was connected and the bodies mysteriously disappeared, you'll be charged as an accomplice," Sam threatened. "You're the one who supposedly examined their bodies and filed bogus reports."

Wilson sat very still. When he finally spoke, his voice was strong and controlled, allowing Sam a glimpse of some small vestige of the man who had once inhabited the now decaying body. "As you may have surmised, Mr. Lerner, I haven't long to live. I have a wife, two children, and one adorable granddaughter. I would appreciate it if you not sully my reputation. That's all I have to show for thirty years of dedication to this thankless job."

"Then talk to me, Wilson."

"I needed money. I have cirrhosis and heart disease. It's an expensive way to die. I don't want to leave my family penniless."

"If you need money for treatment, Wilson, there are other means of getting it."

"It's too late, Mr. Lerner."

"It's not too late to help a mother who needs to say good-bye to her daughter. You must know the importance of saying good-bye."

"I don't know as much as you think. However, I do *believe* the girls drowned." Wilson reached into his drawer, pulled out a bottle of Jack Daniels and drank straight from the bottle. He then pulled out a bottle of Pepto Bismol and washed down a handful of pills with the thick pink liquid.

"Were there indications of anything out of the ordinary when you examined the victims?"

"I don't know about the condition of the bodies," Wilson said into space.

"But you filled out the coroner's reports yourself. You had Madsen's body transported to Whitaker's Funeral Home. And I'm sure a little digging will prove you sent Carol Stone's body there, too."

"Perhaps," Wilson said in a thin voice as he reached back in the drawer. "But I am telling you Mr. Lerner, I am not in any way familiar with the *bodies* of Carol Stone or Madsen Cassaise," he said pointedly.

" 'Not familiar with the bodies'? What the hell does that mean?" Sam paused as he tried to read the coroner's face. "Do you mean the victims' bodies were never even here?"

Wilson turned red and shrugged.

Sam was taken aback. "The bodies of Madsen Cassaise and Carol Stone were never examined by your office?" Sam tried to read Wilson's face as the man took another swig from the bottle.

"People make mistakes. Can't you just let this go?"

"Mistakes? Madsen's body was missing from her own grave. And according to my sources, Carol Stone may not even have a grave. That's a little too coincidental to be a mistake."

"Maybe."

"Did you examine them or not?"

"I guess not."

"What in the hell?" Sam sputtered. "Are you being paid to say you examined deads that were never even brought into your office?"

"I told you I don't know as much as you think."

"Christ, Wilson, so you don't even know if they were dead? They could have been buried alive, for fuck's sake, or used for some sort of bizarre ritual!"

Wilson shuddered and lowered his head. His hands were now shaking uncontrollably. "I don't know how it all came to this, Mr. Lerner. I truly don't. I was once a decent man." After he took another drink of whiskey, he placed the bottle back in the drawer. When he withdrew his hand, he was holding a pistol. He propped one elbow on the desk and pointed the gun directly at Sam.

Sam immediately hit the floor and took cover under the desk. Just as his chair toppled onto the dirty tiles behind him, he heard the click of the safety release on Wilson's weapon.

Sam lunged at Wilson's legs from underneath the desk. "Drop it, Wilson," he yelled as he tried to yank the coroner from his chair. Before Sam could get a firm grip on Wilson, there was an explosion of gunfire followed by the sound of shattering glass. Sam braced his legs and used both arms to shove Wilson away from him. As the chair flew backwards on its casters, Sam lurched upward from under the desk and hurled himself over the desk at Wilson. The chair toppled over with the weight of the two men. When they hit the floor, Wilson lay still, the gun still clenched in his yellowed hand.

Sam stared at a gaping hole that stained Wilson's head like a third eye. The self-inflicted wound oozed blood, draining the last bit of life from the vacant eyes that were fixed on the fluorescent light above.

After he felt for a pulse, Sam gently lowered the waxen arm back onto the floor. He picked up the phone and started to dial, but after a moment, he placed it back in the cradle and walked out.

The suicide was self-evident, and Coroner Wilson would be found soon enough. Notification of a coroner somehow seemed redundant. One thing was sure, Sam figured–Wilson wouldn't need much embalming fluid. His body was fluid enough to be put on tap.

Sam was more concerned about two dead girls. Where were the bodies, and exactly what were their bodies being used for?

Chapter 25

Ramona nervously slipped her fingers under the blond wig to scratch her scalp. While hunched over a table in Tujagues, she kept a constant eye on the front door. The sun was low in the sky, casting long shadows down Decatur Street and distorting the faces of each person who passed by the front window. She wiped her clammy hands on a napkin and looked around the restaurant. When she spotted the elderly man limping toward her, she nodded and held out her hand.

"The waiter said you asked for me," he smiled.

"I'm a friend of Sam Lerner. He told me about you."

"Sam's like my own boy. What can I do for you, dear?" Antoine signaled a waiter to bring a menu.

"I'm not eating, I'm a bit short on money," Ramona apologized.

"You're a friend of Sam's, so you'll pay some other time," Antoine insisted.

"I need to reach Sam. I thought you might know where he is."

"If I did, I'm afraid I couldn't say. I'm sure you understand."

"Well, I was staying with him, and I kinda had to leave in a hurry. I wanted him to know I'm all right."

"Oh, you must be Ramona. Well that changes everything. He sent me out to his place to look for you, but I missed you. He's staying with Maire at the club. Would you like me to run you over there?"

"No, thank you, I can't go there." Ramona tugged at her wig and looked back out at the street. She suddenly spotted a man skulking near the door of a shop several doors down on the opposite side. She was sure he hadn't been there when she arrived. "Can you get a message to Sam? A real confidential one?" she asked.

"Of course."

"You need to warn him. Tell him the guy who was following me showed up out at his house in Chalmette. He was standing in the trees at the edge of the woods, just watchin' the place. The guy is average height, kinda muscular, with dark hair. And tell him I picked up some gossip from the streets. Sam's friend, Leon Duval, was getting oral sex from Charlie Biscay in exchange for the money Charlie needed for rent and stuff. I thought Sam might be interested."

Antoine raised his brows and let out a long whistle.

"Tell Sam I'm leavin' for good," Ramona continued. "I'll contact him once I get where I'm headed."

"Okay, Ramona, I'll see he gets the message," Antoine said as the waiter brought over a bowl of seafood gumbo. "Now relax and eat something."

Ramona looked out the window again. The person in the shadows had disappeared. Keeping her gaze trained on the street, Ramona slowly ate, relishing every bite as if it were her last meal.

Chapter 26

When Ramona hurriedly closed the door behind her, she could see the neon Good Deal Inn sign reflected in the cheap metal cabinet that held the television in her shabby room. Several letters of the sign were burned out, leaving only GO_D illuminated to stand guard over the lonely souls who entered the downtrodden motel in search of refuge. The sign was blinking erratically like a giant sparkler.

Ramona grabbed her suitcase and tossed in the few articles she had unpacked. Standing in front of the vanity, she noticed how pale and thin she had become. Her hands had begun to tremble without warning. It was time for her to get out of town, and she knew it would be dangerous to wait any longer.

Ramona had been trying to locate an old friend in Atlanta to no avail. The money Sam Lerner had lent her was almost gone and would only cover the bus fare and maybe one more night in a cheap place. She would be homeless until the money from the sale of her small stock investment caught up with her, but Ramona had been homeless before.

As she was shoving her remaining belongings into her suitcase, she heard a movement behind her. Ramona reeled around to see if the door lock was firmly in place. Somehow the dead bolt had become slightly askew. Trying to control her panic, she held her breath and moved slowly toward the door.

The sound of heavy breathing registered in her ears just before a rough hand engulfed her neck and squeezed her throat. Before she could scream, another hand covered her mouth. She could taste stale cigar smoke as the fingers mashed her lips against her teeth.

"Hello, Ramona," the voice said from over her shoulder. "If you make a sound, I'll fuck you up so bad you'll beg me to kill you. I SAID hello!"

"Hello, Louis," Ramona rasped through the hard fingers that threatened to crush her face.

"So you didn't know it was me following you?"

"I didn't recognize you," Ramona mumbled. "You cut off your long hair, and you've put on weight since I last saw you."

"Yeah, I've been workin' out," Louis snarled as he violently shoved Ramona onto the bed. He sat down next to her and rubbed his hand along her thigh. "I've been waiting for you. Bathroom windows in hotels are pretty convenient, don't you think?"

Louis pulled out a cigar, bit off the end, and lit a match. After a long pull, he smiled and blew smoke in her face. "So how was dinner at Tujagues, love?"

"Fine, Louis." Ramona's voice cracked as she pushed the words from her bruised throat.

"It's been a long time, sugar."

"Yes, a very long time."

"I was at your place of business a few times. But I thought it best to plan my visits on your days off from whoring. I didn't want to lose the element of surprise when I needed it."

"You did good, Louis. You fooled me."

"You're still a hairy ape," he said as he caressed her arms. And you're looking kinda scrawny. You were a lot hotter to look at when you were working for me in Slidell, eh?" He gave the hair on her arm a hard yank. "Say something, goddamit!"

"I guess I was, Louis. I'm sorry I don't look so good."

"It's okay, baby, I'll fatten you up. You must still be sucking the crack pipe."

"No, I'm clean. Been clean for a long time. And I'm getting out of the business."

"Sure you are. You planning on going back home to set up a a church for hookers? We had a great business in Slidell, you and me. After you split, I went to Baton Rouge and pimped for Madsen and Celeste."

"I didn't know you knew them."

"You don't know much about nothing. They knew better than to ever mention to anyone that they knew me. Anyway, I 'persuaded' Celeste to come here to help me out with my current moneymaking gig. I hit the jackpot when you and Madsen showed up here, too.

"So where is Madsen?"

Louis smiled and leaned close to Ramona's ear. "That's none of your god-damn business! She's with Carol Stone."

"I never heard of her."

"Yes, you have. She had a very brief stint at Maire's place, too. She went by the name of Cara Spencer."

"Cara Spencer? She disappeared! Did you hurt her and Madsen?"

"That's none of your goddamn business either!" Suddenly Louis slapped Ramona hard across the face. Then, with one hand, he yanked the blond wig off her head. Ramona screamed as she felt the attached hair rip away from her scalp. When she lifted her hands to fend off the attack, Louis pulled back his arm and drilled his fist squarely into her stomach.

Ramona rolled off the bed, clutching at her stomach. For several moments the room went black before she managed to suck in a breath over the vomit and blood in her windpipe. She lay on the dank rug, too hurt to move and too exhausted to try. Finally the contents of her stomach forced its way back up again. She detached herself from what was happening and went limp as Louis shoved her onto her back and held a lit cigar over her face.

"You've forgotten a lot since you left me, you skanky whore. You don't ever ask me questions, got it?" While Louis held the cigar close to her face, he felt his erection press against his zipper. When he adjusted his pants, he enjoyed the feel of his own hand against his stiff penis.

Ramona nodded in compliance as she blankly watched the cigar ashes fall toward her face. She could taste the ash as it mixed with her blood and bile.

"Fix your face lovey. Now it's payback time. You can leave your shit here. You won't be needing it."

Ramona rolled to her side again and pushed up onto her hands and knees. She mechanically crawled toward the dresser, her long hair hanging down on both sides as though to shield her from the ugliness of her surroundings. When she reached up for her purse, the contents spilled to the floor, allowing her to retrieve a lipstick. After she flipped the top off with her thumb, she weakly lifted the tube toward her mouth. Still on her hands and knees, Ramona balanced herself on one hand while she applied the lipstick with the other, crushing it against her lips. She licked the wax off her teeth before she looked to Louis for approval.

"You look like Milton Berle," Louis howled derisively. "You're pathetic."

Ramona looked back down at the rug. She wanted to press her head into the fibers, close her eyes, and remain still forever. She knew if she left the room, she would never be seen again. But if she stayed, she'd have to be willing to fight. Either way, she knew she was going to die.

Ramona stared at a dog treat that was lying in a heap on the rug among the contents of her purse. She had bought the piece of rawhide for Beatrice. The tears burned her eyes as her mind tried to distance itself from her overwhelming terror.

Ramona imagined herself lying on Sam Lerner's couch with his dog curled up in a ball on the floor next to her. She could see Sam's shy smile as he walked through the room to the front porch. He looked big as he stood in the door absorbing the sunlight. She believed he would protect her. Somehow he would save her, wouldn't he? Silently she begged him to come.

Louis suddenly pulled her to her feet by her hair and dragged her out the door into the darkness. Ramona stumbled several times as they made their way toward Louis's car. While he yanked the car door open, Ramona spotted a woman watching them from the doorway of an adjacent room. In the recesses of her mind, she recalled seeing the woman at Maire's place. Ramona finally remembered–it was Madsen's mother.

"Get Sam Lerner!" Ramona managed to scream before Louis rammed a fist into her kidney. She doubled over in pain, and when she looked up again, Renee Oleyant was gone.

As Louis shoved Ramona into the car, she fixed her gaze on the neon sign that had given up its watch over the silent motel. Even the GO_D had burned out.

Chapter 27

Sam was sitting on Maire's front porch step when he spotted Renee Oleyant rushing down Ursulines in his direction. He got to his feet as she approached.

"Renee, I thought you went home!"

"Why would I do that?" she asked breathlessly. "I haven't found my daughter, Mr. Lerner."

"I know. And I'm truly sorry. I'm still investigating the matter. Are you okay?"

"Well I came looking for you because I have something urgent to tell you. I saw a man force one of Madsen's friends into his car out at my hotel. I've been trying to track you down ever since."

"What friend? Tell me what happened."

"You know the girl you were talking to that day we met–the brunette with hair down to her knees?"

"Ramona?"

"Yes, I believe that's her name. Last night he dragged her out of the hotel where I'm staying. She looked terrified, and she was beat up pretty badly. He's gonna kill her. I know it."

Sam sat back down on the porch swing with a thud. "Are you sure it was Ramona?" he asked. "My friend Antoine over at Tujagues left word that she was in there last night, and that she was leaving town."

"She got help leaving. He wasn't just a john. He knew her."

"You're positive?"

"As positive as I am that Madsen is finally dead. Your mammy Jem thinks so, too."

"Jem? How do you know Jem?"

"I was sent to her. You may not believe in the signs, Mr. Lerner, but many of us do. I had to know the truth. My daughter may be dead, but I want her body back. I want to lay her to rest properly, and you're the only one who can find her. You bring her back to me. Please. And find Ramona, too. If you were a believer, you would have heard her calling for your help."

Renee Oleyant turned abruptly and headed back up Ursulines. Sam felt completely off-balance as he watched her retreat, her shoulders stooped with the weight of her pain. He tried to catch his breath, but the air in the Big Easy seemed as though it had already been used and discarded.

Chapter 28

"Is that image about right, man?" The kid with yellow steel wool hair interrupted Sam's thoughts while he stood in the middle of Jackson Square watching the artist blow charcoal off the portrait he had just sketched. Sam nodded, handed the kid twenty dollars, and studied the sketch. The profile of the stranger he had spotted at Tujagues, and who likely was the bastard who had assaulted him, looked even meaner when rendered in charcoal. Sam carefully rolled the sketch and headed for the car, sidestepping several mimes and a fortune teller in a wench getup that was a showstopper.

Joe had called him from L.A. right after he left the Coroner's Office. He told Sam he had finally come up with names and descriptions of three Louisiana criminals using 'The Saint' as an alias. Sam found one ex-con particularly intriguing. Joe mentioned a guy named Louis Santos who had a rap sheet that should have made parole a felony.

Louis Santos was thirty-nine and had been in trouble all his life. He had forged checks, pimped in many cities, racked up two counts of assault with a deadly, and had gotten off on a murder rap only because two key witnesses had disappeared. And he had been doing business out of Baton Rouge where Madsen had most recently been living.

Although Joe was going to send him a screenshot of the mug photos, Sam had asked the artist to do a sketch from his own description for an objective comparison with the images Joe was sending. Sam wanted to positively identify Santos as the same guy who had been on his tail, the reason for which was still unclear to Sam. He also asked Joe to fax the mug sheet to a local copy center so he could see it enlarged.

With sketch in hand, Sam got into Maire's car and started the engine. He could smell Maire's scent all around him, making him anxious to be back in her bed. Maire was the one person he felt he could count on, and he suddenly wanted her more than ever. He thought about her as he drove the several blocks to the copy center.

As he exited the car, he saw a black Chevrolet Impala SS disappear into an alley just north of the business. Sam hesitated. He was about to head inside when he saw the nose of the car ease back out of the alley then suddenly come to a halt.

Sam started toward the alley, but changed his mind. Without his weapon, he felt as vulnerable as a blond boy on a death row cell block. Instead, he turned and entered the store.

A woman in Rasta dreadlocks set down her sandwich and made her way to him in slow motion. She leaned on the counter and waited for him to state his business. Her eyes were dilated, and her focus shifted around Sam's head as if she were tracking his aura.

"Have you received a fax from the Los Angeles Police Department?" Sam asked, keeping his gaze on the window. The woman nodded to the counter.

When Sam looked down, Louis Santos glared back up at him from the page. He looked thinner than he was now, but he had the same jaw line and head cock Sam remembered. And his profile matched the sketch the artist had drawn from Sam's description. Joe had scrawled on the bottom of the page: "Santos recently beat a rap after one woman failed to testify on a rape and sodomy charge. She had been brutalized. This misunderstood individual likes S & M devices and weapons. And fish. Watch your back, buddy."

Sam took out his phone and dialed while making copies of the photo. "It's Sam," he said into the phone when Joe picked up. "I got your fax. What do you mean about the fish? You mean he collects fish, or he dates 'em?"

"Well, the kinky douche probably does both, but he's definitely an aficionado of scaly things. He had seven aquariums in his pad the last time he was busted. His landlady complained about the dead eels she found in the trash."

"Thanks, man. I had a hunch. Catch you later."

Sam held out a bill to the clerk, who was studying her lunch as if it were a work of art. The woman took a bite out of a peach and continued to chew long after she had swallowed it. She seemed unfazed by the peach juice that ran down her wrist, coating her tattoo of Ziggy Marley.

After a beat, Sam left the bill on the counter and headed for the door. "That must be some good shit. Have another bong load, sweetheart," he called over his shoulder to the clerk, who was too busy communicating with her sandwich to notice his departure.

As Sam jumped into the car and turned toward the aquarium, he could see the Chevy Impala pull out of the alley and turn in the same direction.

"You've been up my ass like a love sick gerbil!" Sam said into his rear view mirror. "Exactly what are you up to, Duval?"

* * *

During the short drive to the aquarium, Sam kept an eye on Duval, who was maintaining a one block distance as he tailed Sam in what was obviously a borrowed car.

After Sam parked, he got out and showed photocopies of Louis Santos to the street musicians in the area while chatting with each one. He shot occasional glances toward the Chevy, which had slipped between two trucks parked on the street.

As he returned to the car, Sam stopped abruptly to retrieve an object from the ground. When he looked up, he made direct eye contact with Duval, who grinned sheepishly before giving a polite nod.

"Just checking to see who was driving Maire's car," Duval called innocently from the driver's side window, "I thought it might have been stolen. You stay safe, and stay out of trouble. Remember, you're a person of interest." He shoved the Chevy into drive and stuck his hand out the window as he pulled out of the lot. Before he rounded the curb, Duval held up his forefinger and shook it at Sam.

Sam caught the gesture. "That better mean 'see you later,' you redneck bubba."

When Sam got back into the car, he looked at the photo of Louis Santos. Sam had correctly suspected that "The Saint," the sadistic fish aficionado of Baton Rouge, would likely be a frequent visitor to the New Orleans' Aquarium. A musician outside the aquarium had told him that a guy who matched the artist's sketch often dropped by on weekday afternoons.

Sam pulled out the Esplendido cigar butt he had retrieved from the parking lot and studied it. It was just a matter of time before he and Santos would meet again. Perhaps it was time to retrieve his weapon. But first, he needed Maire.

Chapter 29

Sam drummed his fingers against Maire's headboard as he stared at the moonlight shadows. He and Maire had feasted on a scrumptious dinner at Muriel's on St. Ann's in Jackson Square. The pork chops were the best he had ever had, but he still had a craving or two. He wanted a drink again. The need just wouldn't go away, and the recent gifts of beer and Cuervo from Duval had only increased his struggle.

Did Duval want him to stay loaded, Sam wondered? Drunks are sloppy. They overlook a lot, and their information is not considered dependable. Perhaps that was what Duval was counting on. Sam may have returned to town in the middle of something that had progressed too far to stop, and thus, Duval had to deal with his old cop friend without tipping him off. Was Sam the bone that was to keep the dog occupied while the boys broke into the junkyard? If so, what were Duval and his boys up to?

Sam was pondering Duval's motivations when Maire sashayed in, backlit by the rosy glow in the hallway. He took one look at her and shoved aside his thoughts about Duval and anything else that didn't involve Maire.

"Maire," he whispered into the dark. "You look really great in that white thing."

Maire laughed softly. "It's a sarong, and thank you, chere."

"One more blow to my skull and I won't be able to get any words out at all." Sam draped an arm over Maire as she lay down on the bed next to him. His other arm was propped over his forehead, holding back the dull headache that was now part of his anatomy. He was wearing nothing but a cotton robe as he tried to release the tension of the day. "I think Ramona's in trouble," he said quietly.

"I think you are, too, chere," she said as she rubbed his temples. "You're in too deep. Ramona can take care of herself. She's a street kid. It's time for you to move on."

"You're always kicking me out of bed," he teased. He could feel her body heat when she moved closer to him.

"Not this time. I just want you to be safe," Maire said softly while brushing her lips against his ear. "I decided to take something I want before you go." Maire lay her head on Sam's bare chest and kissed his damp skin, burying her face in his dark chest hair.

As Sam held Maire close to him, he breathed in deeply. He could feel himself growing harder at the same time he was fighting his urge to flee. "I really want you, Maire," he whispered, "but I don't know if I can deal with it, and you should know I don't plan on staying."

"I know, but I'll be okay. Let me help you forget everything that's happened, Sam."

He knew what she meant. It wasn't Madsen, or Ramona, or his recent assault to which she was referring. Maire wanted to fill the empty space left by the losses in his life. And Sam had discovered that empty spaces can be very heavy.

For a brief moment Sam thought of Ramona and Madsen again. He felt guilty for having human needs while other people were depending upon him. He knew he had to find them. But first he had to find himself.

Sam smiled at Maire. "I'm afraid my head will fall off."

"I'm interested in the other parts. I can work around it," she said, smiling back.

When Maire moved her mouth farther down his chest to his smooth, hard stomach, Sam's muscles flexed to her touch. Suddenly he realized that all the years they had known each other had been leading to this moment. That had danced around it forever, partially to protect their friendship, and mostly because they both sensed that their time had not come.

Their time was now, and they both knew it. He was in her bed because he had nowhere else to go. And no place better that he wanted to be. Sam always knew Maire could either heal him or destroy him. And right now he needed healing. He had nothing left to lose.

With one hand, Maire pulled his robe apart. Sam's body sought her as she licked the skin just above his pelvis. He could feel her breath on his thighs as she moved farther down. His body shuddered. Sam slowly gave in, sinking further into the sheets.

He let out a low moan as Maire's tongue further awakened him. He felt as if all of his being was centered in his aching groin. He wanted more, so much so that he was afraid to exhale. Then Sam closed his eyes while Maire's warm mouth covered him, taking him to places he had long since forgotten.

Chapter 30

Duval sat in his car watching the docks. He reflected on his recent mistakes, but he knew he could cover his ass just like he always did when he miscalculated. He just needed to make sure he kept tabs on Sam.

It hadn't been too hard to trace his old buddy's recent whereabouts. He had seen Sam's pooch lying around when he had dropped by Maire's place for a little money-exchange. Duval also knew that Ramona Slocum had been holed up at Sam's farm in Chalmette. What he had underestimated was Sam's ongoing hard-on for Maire. He figured Sam would have moved on by now, until he realized Sam was clinging to a past that was a lot more carefree than the shit he had been through up in L.A. *I hear ya on that one, Buddy*, he thought. But maybe this was a good thing after all. He could use Sam to protect himself.

Duval had just missed Sam at Charlie's home out at the bayou. He had suspected Sam would go there in search of Charlie, and Duval wanted to make sure Charlie gave up no secrets. Duval had let a personal revelations slip around Charlie, and the nosy old queen always asked too damn many questions anyway. Unfortunately, Duval was too late to know if Charlie talked, or to even say good-bye. He sure would miss the colorful ol' queer.

In some respects, Duval was relieved Charlie was dead. Charlie had begun to rot in front of him, and the poor guy's physical pain was frightening to watch. Hopefully Charlie took his memories to the grave with him, particularly those of trading Duval blow jobs for rent money and meds. He would be humiliated if Sam were ever to find out. But Duval would miss Charlie. Charlie was one of the few people who could make him laugh after he and Linny split up.

Upon leaving Charlie's plantation, he had stopped at the bayou market. Jeb, the old salt who ran the place, said he had overheard Sam on the phone talking to someone about Cat's Blues Heaven. That seemed like an odd choice now that Sam was back on the wagon. What was Sam up to, he wondered?

"I asked you to help me, Sammy," he mumbled aloud, "but I ain't gonna let you steal the limelight. Now you're just getting in my way."

Chapter 31

Ramona's prayers had become a silent incantation. "Please God, let me die now," she begged. The oily gag in her mouth allowed for little air, giving her hope she might suffocate. Anything would be better than what Louis Santos said he had planned for her.

With hands and feet tightly bound, Ramona had no hope of escape. And she was afraid to open her eyes again. The last time she had looked out the car window, she had seen Louis standing near the dock talking to a man whose face reminded her of a drawing she had made of the devil when she was four years old. In the moonlight, his skin looked as though it had melted in the fires of his Hell.

With one last hope for survival, Ramona willed her eyes to open again. Louis and the man with the scarred face were standing over a box that lay on the ground, its top propped open like a large mouth waiting to be fed. Ramona knew she was to be its repast.

Ramona screamed into her gag. As she struggled once more to free her hands, a face suddenly loomed over her. She cried out at the sight of the pale apparition, but when she recognized the face, she grew still, comforted by the bawdy blond image of Celeste, who was staring blankly at her through the car window. As Ramona's head flopped puppet-like against the seat, she sobbed with relief.

Celeste, however, made no attempt to free her. Instead, she turned her back on Ramona and called out Louis's name.

"No," Ramona cried into the filthy cloth that restricted her jaw. She believed there would be no hope for escape if Louis were to spot Celeste before she could set Ramona free. As her tormentor turned to squint in the direction of the voice, Ramona trembled in terror. Celeste, however, did not back away.

"Did you think you could cut me out of our deal, you prick?" she whispered menacingly. "After all the shit you put me through?"

"Now, Celeste-"

"Shut up!" Celeste ordered as Louis slowly approached. Ramona pressed her back farther into the seat, confused by the strange power Celeste seemed to have over the man. Louis was approaching slowly, his hands held aloft to convey a nonthreatening demeanor. Before Louis reached Celeste, the other man with the devil face turned and ran, disappearing behind the oil drums that lined the wharf.

Slowly Celeste raised her arm. Moonlight glinted off a metal object in her hand. "You're close enough for me to customize your twisted brain," Celeste laughed derisively, "I like courage in a man. Even an ugly, miserable dead one."

"You don't mean that, baby-"

"Didn't I tell you to shut up? I'm doing the talking now you fucking freak! I kept my end of the bargain. You knew which girls had no families, and you got an exact report of their whereabouts so you could work your sick little scheme. Now I want what's mine."

"You dumb bitch, you didn't earn shit!" Louis snapped. Madsen *has* a relative, Celeste. She has a mother who almost fucked up the whole scheme!"

"That wasn't my fault. Madsen lied about having any family who might come looking. I told you about Carol Stone, didn't I? You're the one who blew that one, Louis. You were supposed to drug them long enough to transport them, not kill them. Can't you do anything right?"

"I'll get this one right, baby," he said pushing out his lower lip in a pseudo pout as he nodded toward the car.

Ramona shook her head back and forth violently as Louis took another step closer.

"That's far enough, big boy," Celeste cautioned. "I know you received a hefty sum up front. Toss me my share now, and I'll just walk away. We can pretend as if none of this ever went down. You get Ramona, and I walk away without talking."

Celeste turned to look at Ramona. She almost felt sorry for the captive girl who was screaming silently into the filthy gag. Ramona's eyes met hers, and then she suddenly recoiled.

Celeste saw Louis's reflection in the car window just as he charged her from behind.

Chapter 32

Louis Santos watched the women from a distance as they danced in a clearing deep in Black Bayou outside Houma. As he hovered among the moss-laden cypress trees, he was mesmerized by the fire in the center of the circle. The flames jumped upward to lick the sky, scattering sparks into the breeze like thousands of fireflies. Louis's heart beat faster as his feelings alternated between hypnotic attraction and a vague sense of threat.

The sound of drums that pounded in his ears were accompanied by lilting voices and cries of ecstasy. Young initiates in white cotton dresses, worn sandals, and twisted kerchiefs danced in a circle and cried out repeatedly as they communed with the spirits. Their voices, saturated with dank bayou air, lingered over the nearby swamp before disappearing into the night.

Slowly the fervor of the voodoo ceremony increased and a frenzy spread through the crowd. One girl swooned, as if drained of all life. She fell backwards into outstretched arms while others moved in to take her place.

The priestess lifted her face toward the fog-draped moon and called out prophesies in a voice that was high-pitched and almost inhuman. Louis quietly moved closer for a better view. He grinned and licked his lips in anticipation of what was to come.

The ground reverberated with the pounding of feet. As it reached a crescendo, the priestess shoved her hand into a cage and pulled out a chicken. She stretched the head of the bird away from its neck and held it over her head as she danced. After she wiped the bird across her sweat soaked brow, she grabbed a knife from the fire. With one quick movement, she sliced the chicken's neck.

As the crowd gasped, the priestess bit into the bird's flesh. She squeezed the carcass, increasing the flow of blood, and then she swung the chicken over her head, spraying the crowd with the chicken blood. The dancers were now spinning about the fire, their gyrations growing more spastic and sexual while they drove themselves into a state of rapture.

Louis watched through eyes bleary and bloodshot from a variety of mind-altering drugs. Sweat ran down his back, but the familiar rush of desire made him shiver. Slowly he leaned back and began to tug at his erect penis. As his breathing increased, so did his frustration at his failure to bring himself to orgasm. He stroked himself more vigorously and moaned aloud as the women pressed their damp bodies against each other. Gradually Louis's fevered body and fractured mind became one, and his power felt limitless.

Louis was startled by the grasp of a firm hand on his shoulder and the sharp jab of a thumb digging into his back. "You be putting your member back in your trousers now," the woman ordered, in a voice tinted with French dialect, "or we do no business."

Louis swore under his breath as he felt his erection rapidly diminish. After a beat, he wiped his mouth with the back of his hand. Then, with a perverse grin, he took his time stuffing himself back into his pants in order to make sure she could appraise his manhood.

"Well well, Micheline," he oozed, "did you bring my supply?" He rubbed his testicles, leaned back against the tree, and fixed his gaze on her turban. He was enthralled by its bright colors that swirled like a lava lamp before receding into the night.

"You look at me," Micheline demanded in an attempt to direct his focus. "I heard you were careless," she whispered. "You were warned that puffer fish tetrodotoxin is more lethal than cyanide. And now, I hear someone is dead, eh?"

Louis shrugged. "Maybe," he sneered, "so what's the big deal about a hooker or two?"

"I want no part of that business."

"Relax. I think I'll get the dose right with the next one. But now I need a new supply."

"The risk of contributing to your 'profession' is too high. You bring dark energy."

"Ah, but that's why your pay-off is big."

"Then I assume my reward will be bigger this time?"

"We've already set a price," Louis snapped.

"The price has changed since your barge captain accomplice was here."

Louis pushed his face closer to Micheline's. "Yeah? What did that freak face Faustin want with a zombie specialist like you?"

"Treatment for the facial burns you gave him," Micheline said, meeting his stare. "He told me how you botched your last "shipment," and he said he heard that a man named Sam Lerner is interested in your transactions."

"Lerner is nobody."

"You don't know much, Mr. Santos. Sam Lerner is a cop with a reputation, even down here. He was a football star at Tulane. He knows people, and he can persuade folks to talk. His mammy was a high priestess in Haiti. If anyone sees me with you, it could get back to her. This new set of circumstances increases my risk, and therefore my price."

"Sam Lerner is past his prime; and I've put the fear of Louis Santos in him. If he doesn't leave town soon, he'll be worse off than Faustin. What's that's old expression, 'Fight fire with fire'?"

Louis suddenly flicked his lighter and shoved it toward Micheline. She gasped and backed away holding her hands up to protect her face. Louis laughed and then extinguished the flame. "So you get only the amount of money we discussed," he said menacingly as he pulled out a roll of bills. "You got any more complaints?"

Micheline eyed the wad of money. Without counting it, she grabbed the bills and stuffed them into her waistband. I'll have another supply tomorrow night. "Remember, use a camphor and ammonia mixture to awaken the victim the way I told you. Be exact with this medicine. And don't be comin' back here after I deliver the rest!" She gave him a dark look before turning away.

"You better deliver! And nice doin' business with you," Louis taunted. As she moved silently toward the other voodoo dancers, the drum beat grew loud again.

Louis watched a moment longer. He looked around to make sure he was not being followed before he slipped away. Micheline glanced back to see only a black smear disappear amidst the shadows of the bayou.

Chapter 33

Sam sat in the aquarium parking lot, fearful he was running out of time. He had to find Santos. No one had heard from Ramona for two days. He had asked his friend Joe to track down Ramona's sister in Atlanta for him. According to the sister, Ramona had never arrived. Santos had taken Ramona from the motel, but was she still alive, he wondered?

Sam was now involved in solving Madsen's disappearance, whether he liked it or not. And Ramona was the next victim. He needed help, but not the kind he was getting from Duval. Duval had lured him in, yet he was thwarting him at every crooked turn. He suspected Duval didn't give a rat's ass about a few missing call girls. But if Sam could help him out while taking no glory, maybe Duval could get that promotion he wanted. It also occurred to him that Duval could have something to lose if the investigation went too far. However, Duval would expect his old buddy to look the other way if Sam were to stumble onto something that could implicate Duval. Cronyism was thicker in these parts than Spanish moss.

"Bingo," Sam said aloud when he finally spotted Santos "I've got you now, you fucker."

When Santos brushed past a strolling violinist on his way to the parking area, Sam surreptitiously gave a thumbs-up to the musician. The musician nodded and continued to play. Sam then slipped down in the driver's seat and waited for Santos to pull out of the parking lot before he started his car and began to tail him. Sam knew his rented Chevy was much less conspicuous than the Shelby, but he remained a safe distance behind.

"This time we do it my way, pal," Sam said as they moved along the river front. Once they passed the horse-drawn carriages that moseyed through the tourist areas, Santos picked up speed.

They had passed through Chalmette on the St Bernard Highway into Meraux when Santos turned onto a dirt road near the railroad tracks and headed closer to the river. Sam passed him in order not to draw attention, and then he made a U-turn as soon as possible and backtracked. He followed the trail of road dust until the road came to an end.

When he saw Santos park near what appeared to be an abandoned storage building between the tracks and the river, Sam pulled over behind a group of trees. From his vantage point, Sam could see Santos approach the entrance of the building and peer over his shoulder before turning the key and stepping inside.

After a few moments, Sam excited his vehicle and slipped through the trees, careful to stay as out of view as possible. As he crept alongside the small ramshackle building, he observed the peeling paint on its thick cinder block walls. The windows of the structure were opaque, many of them cracked and stained with age.

Sam tried the side door, but the padlock held firm. When he noticed a gap in the broken glass of an adjacent window, he used his thumbnail to pull a shard of the glass toward him, careful that the rest of the window did not give way. The enlarged crack allowed for a slim field of vision. Once he adjusted his eyes, Sam had a fractured image of what was going on inside the mostly empty space.

At first, Sam observed nothing but a shabby room. Then Santos stepped into view. Sam watched as Santos pushed a coffin-like box closer to the entrance door and removed the cover. The box appeared to be cheap and rough-hewn like the one Sam had seen on the river front the night he was mugged.

Santos then dragged a tarp toward the box. The tarp was partially out of view, but Sam could see it contained a bundle and was covered with tape. Removing a knife from his pocket, Santos cut the tape on the tarp. When the tarp fell open, Sam was taken aback. A leg protruded from the tarp and hit the floor in shocking finality. Sam squinted until he could make out the tattoo on the woman's calf. It was a fleur de lis. An inexplicable sadness came over him as he realized the lifeless body belonged to Celeste.

Santos removed Celeste's watch and shoved it into his pocket. Sam was sure he had seen vultures approach carnage with more respect than this maggot of a human being.

"I told you I'm the boss, Celeste. You had it good with me, bitch," Santos sneered. Sam got a glimpse of her face as Santos struggled to stuff Celeste's bruised body into the box. Judging from the accusing hole in her forehead and her blood-matted hair, her cause of death had been a bullet wound. But her battered body had obviously been used and abused before death was kind enough to release her.

Santos threw the tarp in on top of her and then slammed the lid closed. "Did you really think *you* could shoot Louis Santos, you tramp?"

Sam was contemplating his next move when he heard an almost indistinguishable voice. "Please," someone pleaded. The voice was weak, and the terror was palpable. "Let me go."

Startled, Santos pulled out a gun and reeled around in the direction of the voice. He hesitated, and then he lowered his weapon and spoke to someone out of Sam's view. "Oh, so we're finally conscious, are we? Well, bitch, you'll be sleeping again soon enough."

"Please," the voice begged.

"Shut up. I'm taping up your pie hole again. I don't need to hear your whimpering."

"No," she cried.

Sam finally distinguished the voice. It was Ramona.

* * *

Sam was contemplating his next move. He thought he could take Santos, but Santos still had his weapon in hand. He could see that the door of the storage building was locked from the inside, so he waited for an advantage, which came when Santos placed his weapon on the lid of Celeste's coffin and pulled out his cell phone.

After a pause, Santos barked into the phone, "Listen up you ghoul. I'm gonna mark one box with an 'x.' The cargo in that one gets dumped after you leave the harbor. That's the dead cargo. As always, bring back the box. I'll need it. Do it where you dumped those other bodies. And don't confuse the boxes, you fuck. The other box will have the live shipment."

Santos pulled a pen out of his jacket pocket and drew an 'x' while he listened to the person on the other end of the call. Suddenly he kicked the box and yelled into the phone. "How the hell should I know? It was a simple error. They're *supposed* to look dead, moron. It's the price of doing business. I've got to prepare the next one tonight. It oughta work this time. She'll be catatonic until she's out of port and on the way to Cuba."

Sam heard Ramona moan. Santos reached out and smacked her hard. Sam could barely contain himself when he heard the sickening blow. While Santos had his back turned, Sam grabbed an old rag off the ground. He wrapped it tightly around his hand for protection before carefully pulling a large shard of glass free from the window, praying the glass would not give way. He let out his breath when the remaining pieces clung to the frame like yellowed shark's teeth.

Santos lost his patience and spit out more orders to his accomplice. "Listen up! She'll be like a zombie. Then once you meet our connection and open the box, administer the stuff I gave you just the way I directed, and then the broad will come 'round once you're out of port. Micheline says you have a few hours, and she knows her shit. No worries about noise or escape en route like our merchandise from the past. 'Why'? 'Why'? Because I'm the fucking brains and you work for me! Just get here early so we can move our merchandise out on time. There's big bucks in this for us!"

Santos shoved his phone into his pocket, grabbed his weapon, and headed for the door. "I'll be back soon," he said as he looked back in Ramona's direction. "Then you'll get to take a long nap in a very nice coffin." His ominous laugh echoed off the cinder block walls as he yanked open the door.

Sam was ready. As Santos withdrew his key and bent forward to lock the door of the storage building behind him, Sam rushed him. Santos, still holding his gun, turned just as Sam reached the door. With the coil-and-spring instincts of a rattle snake, Santos raised his weapon.

Sam knew he'd have to kill Santos or die. He chose to live. With one clean swing, he knocked the weapon from the burly man's hand, and then he buried the glass shard deep into his thick neck. The neck seemed to explode, bathing them both in a burst of blood. Sam looked down at Santos, who stared at him in shock. "Die, you motherfucker," he muttered.

He retrieved Santos's gun and shoved the dying man away from the entrance. With weapon in hand, he forced the door open and stepped into hell.

Chapter 34

Ramona had passed out, her head tilted awkwardly to one side. Sam felt for a pulse before gingerly pulling the tape away from her mouth. Celeste's coffin lay nearby, so he instinctively pushed away the lid and reached in. Pressing his fingers against her neck, he felt only the stillness of death.

He scanned the interior of the room. The walls were coated with a film of dirt and oil; and the pervasive stench of fish was sickening. Several battered chairs were flush against the wall as if refusing to gaze upon the ugliness of the surroundings. There were traces of blood on the floor along with a collection of debris, ropes and bloody bungee cords. Rolls of duct tape and blood-stained rags were piled near the door.

A stained laundry sink, vanity and toilet had been installed in one corner with no partition. "I'll get you some water," he said as he turned back toward Ramona, who was still unresponsive. Several rats scattered at the sound of his voice. It was then that he spotted another crude crate in the opposite corner.

Sam approached slowly, fearing what he might find inside. The top of the crate had not yet been sealed, so he was able to pry the lid off with his hands. He breathed a sigh of relief when he saw that the crate was empty. It was then that he noticed the inside of the lid. It had been scratched numerous times. The scratches were not deep, but he could see flecks of silver plate embedded in several grooves in the wood, along with bits of dried blood and flesh, and traces of a waxy, perfumed substance. A wave of nausea gripped Sam's stomach as he ran his fingers along the marks that were a last message to anyone who could hear. But no one had heard. In his gut he knew the silver plate was from a necklace. "Madsen," he whispered, "forgive me for being too late, my friend."

* * *

Sam looked down at his phone. No signal. Fucking AT&T. He knew he had to revive Ramona and get her out of there before he could drive to a more mobile-friendly location. "Hold on, Ramona," he yelled. "It's all over. You're safe now."

Sam rushed to the sink in the corner to look for a container to hold water. He was revolted when he saw a stack of photos on the sink, each one displaying the image of a naked young woman who was tied and gagged. How many victims had there been? When he opened the vanity below the sink, the details of Santos's sick crimes started to come together for him.

The first thing he spotted was the dirty syringes and IV tubes. He held up an empty vial and read the label. Propofol, a powerful drug used for anesthesia. So that's how the bastard kept them quiet until he was ready to ship his "merchandise."

What he withdrew from the cabinet next stunned him. A very small vial of liquid was marked in handwriting so small he had to squint to read it. Tetrodotoxin. As a fisherman, he recognized the word. Tetrodotoxin was a lethal poison found in puffer fish. He knew that some people in countries like Brazil still ate the fish, gambling their lives on proper cleaning and extraction of the poison. Acute poisoning with the neurotoxin caused organs and breathing to shut down, and victims were reported to have gone into catatonic states before almost inevitable death. Supposedly a few people had survived when treated in time, and when breathing assist had been given almost immediately. But very few.

Sam had heard rumors of the neurotoxin being used by practitioners of dark voodoo in archaic rituals, which had given a bad name to those who honored the traditions of ancestor worship and African spiritual folkways. He suspected the poison had come from one of the few remaining groups who practiced dark magic. And it couldn't get much darker than this.

Sam quickly connected the dots. Santos and his accomplices were trafficking humans. Their crude plan was to keep them drugged and captive in crates until ready for shipment, and then they would administer the tetrodotoxin to render them catatonic until they were safely en route and less likely to be discovered. If the coffin-like boxes were randomly inspected, the victims would truly appear dead, as breathing and pulse rate would be almost undetectable. "One problem, you piece of human filth," Sam muttered aloud, "their chance of survival would be minimal at best. Someone sold you a lie along with the tetro, and you fell for it."

Santos had fucked up bigtime. Sam now knew Madsen was dead and that her body had been dumped, probably somewhere at sea, and probably Carol Stone had met the same fate. Maybe death had allowed them to escape an even worse fate that was awaiting them at the destination point, but Sam nonetheless felt a crushing sadness. "Goddamit," he yelled as he fought the urge to ram his fist into the wall.

Sam hurriedly rinsed out an empty soda bottle and filled it with water for Ramona. Suddenly a shot of adrenalin shot up his spine as his senses alerted him to the presence of a predator. Before he could pull his weapon and turn around, a violent blow connected to the back of his head. A hollow sound registered in his brain, and then the room went dark.

Chapter 35

An aching pressure pushed at the edges of Sam's skull. When he tried to lift his arm to rub his temple, he was unable to move. After he managed to force open his eyes, he had to blink several times in order to focus. The light in the room was low, but Sam quickly determined that he was confined to a chair. Each of his wrists was taped to a chair arm, and each ankle was taped to the chair in the same manner. He couldn't remember where he was or how he got there until he heard a familiar voice seep through the web of confusion in his brain.

"I'm sorry about the restraints, Sammy," the voice said. "I did you a solid and didn't gag you cuz there ain't no one close to here anyway. I'll get you some water."

Sam turned his head, a move that sent a shot of pain down his neck and into his shoulder blade. When he spotted a woman tied to another chair, the details of location and circumstance etched their way back into his consciousness. Ramona was still slumped over, but she appeared to be breathing. "She's okay, the voice said from behind him. "Just resting for now."

As Sam tried to move, the rickety chair swayed a bit but held him fast. "What the fuck," he mumbled. When a large hand shoved a bottle of water in front of him, Sam looked up. A remorseful grimace had plastered itself onto the face of Leon Duval.

"Damn, I'm sorry buddy," he apologized. "I shouldn't have dragged you into this, but I thought you could appease that Oleyant woman when she showed up out of nowhere. I knew you'd do your own investigating regardless, so I thought it would be better if I could just keep tabs on you."

Duval nodded toward one corner where Santos's bleeding corpse lay in a heap. "I dragged him inside because, well, because he didn't make a good door stop. He was supposed to follow you, not use your skull like a piñata. What an asshole."

Duval shook his head in frustration. "You know man, I could have focused the investigation on you, seeing as you were one of the last people to see Madsen alive, but I protected you. I'm not all bad, even though you may be thinkin' different right about now."

"Who are you trying to convince, me or yourself?"

"Seriously, when the shit hit the fan, I probably should have framed you. At least it wouldn't have come to this."

While Sam stared in disbelief, Duval paced the floor and then removed a handkerchief from his pocket and blew his nose before speaking again. "It all would have gone away quickly if that mother hadn't shown up to throw a wrench in the works. Jesus, we even faked a burial and got a grave marker, but even that didn't keep her off my ass. But you coulda convinced her it was all taken care of without pokin' that far into things that weren't your business. And now look where we're at." Duval shoved the hankie back into his pocket and kicked an empty bottle on the floor. "Goddamit it Sammy, you've forced my hand!"

Sam slowly pieced the shards of his memory back together. This asshole was working with Santos. He glanced around at the wooden crates that had been pushed toward the door. Madsen and Celeste are dead, he remembered. He looked over at Ramona once more. She was still alive, but for how long?

"You were a good cop, Sammy. So you know I can't let you tell anyone about all this. I just wanted to tell you I feel bad, cuz this was only supposed to involve some whores, and not an old pal like you. I'll take care of your pooch, so no worries there."

Sam thought Duval's hangdog expression would have been pathetic had he not been staring down at his weapon. He knew what Duval was telling him, and he needed to buy some time. "You move silently for a Neanderthal," Sam muttered.

"Yeah, well the water was running and you were pretty intent on saving her, so I had a bit of an advantage." Duval nodded his head toward Ramona. "They're just prostitutes, Sam. They're girls who sell themselves. They would be doing the same thing where we were sending them, so it's no big loss. And nobody was supposed to die. There's a lot of money involved. I make my cut mostly by looking the other way and paying off a few people, like the rotting coroner and that funeral director slimeball. It's a mutually beneficial arrangement."

"'Mutually beneficial'? You can't really believe that!"

"You know, you could look the other way, too, Sammy. Ya think you could do that for a really nice chunk of change?" Duval's eyes met Sam's for a moment, before he looked down again. "No, I guess not. You're too damn much of a Boy Scout."

"You actually think because these girls are escorts that trafficking them is justified?" Sam squeezed his hand into a fist and tried to lift it, but his arm was taped tight to the wobbly chair. "Your pervert partner Santos was selling them as sex-slaves. And you allowed it, you scumbag."

"Aw, Sammy, you don't know what life is like in the Big Easy nowadays. I ain't getting' rich, and no one is going to miss those whores anyway. We made sure they were loners. And now that my Linny is gone, I just need enough money to retire in Cuba–got connections there. But you've gone and complicated everything. I'm gonna have to get these gals outta here by myself tonight. And I guess you know I'm gonna have do something about you, too."

The shame on Duval's face seemed almost genuine. "Here, he said, offering Sam the bottle of water. "I don't want you to die thinking I'm all bad. I'm just practical, buddy."

As Duval leaned into Sam, Sam suddenly slammed his head into Duval's face with such impact that Duval reeled backwards. Instinctively, he came back at Sam with a blow to Sam's upper body, knocking the chair over. Sam hit the floor with great force, which was exactly the result he wanted. The old chair split into pieces, with Sam still taped to its brittle wood members.

Sam was able to lift his arm just as Duval was coming at him again. In one swift movement, he swung at Duval's face, taking the big man down. Duval's weapon slid across the floor toward Sam as if drawn by a magnet. Sam opened his fist, seized the weapon, and blew a hole in Duval's chest.

Shock registered on Duval's face as he felt the shot connect with his ribs. "Christ, Sammy," he whispered, "that's why you were a great quarterback. You could always knew how to call the next play."

* * *

Here's my next play, Duval," Sam said as he yanked the tape off his arms with his teeth. "I'm going to get Ramona some help. And you can just rot here until you die or those rats eat your fucking eyes out."

Duval followed Sam's nod toward several rodents that were chewing on a candy wrapper near the sink. Panic stretched across his face when he eyed the blood stain now crawling across his shirt. "No Sam, you can't leave me. Please. I'm terrified of rats. They'll smell the blood and come after me. If nothing else, just drag me outside!"

"No can do. You'll get about as much mercy from me as you gave those girls." Sam moved closer to Ramona and felt for a pulse. "Thank God she's still alive."

"Yes, but not for long. You need to call the paramedics now, or it will be your fault if she dies." Duval's breathing was becoming more labored, and his eyes continuously darted toward the corner where the rats were gathered.

"No need. I'm taking her with me."

"No, Sammy. C'mon, please. I'm sorry for everything. Give me another chance. I can make things right. Just get me out of here."

"Can you make this right?" Sam walked toward a crate and jerked the lid off. Celeste stared back at him with lifeless eyes. "I'm going to seal you in one of these boxes so when your barge captain comes, he can take you with him. I'll give you some of the tetro. You won't be able to call for help. You'll lose control of your limbs, but you'll know you've been buried alive. Then I'll throw in a few furry creatures to keep you company. You can think about what parts of your body they're feasting on while you pray for death."

"Sam, I'm begging you. I'm not afraid to die. But please, not that way."

"Your victims had no choice, so you don't get to choose either Duval."

"Just shoot me for chrissake!"

Sam walked over to Duval and patted him down. Duval was bleeding out and too weak to move. When Sam found his cell phone, Duval smiled. "Yes, please get help. Hurry."

"Not yet. You think I don't know you'll lie to your good-ol-boy cronies about what's gone down here? You're going to tell me everything if you want to live, Duval. Every fucking detail. If you're still alive after your confession, then maybe I'll call for help."

"Aw Sammy, do you know what they'll do to a cop like me if I go to prison?"

"You'll get all the sex favors you want, big guy. Just like you got by manipulating Charlie. So it wouldn't be all bad, right?"

Duval winced with embarrassment and then started to choke. Sam propped him up so he could breathe better. Duval began sobbing just as Sam pushed the Record button on the phone.

Chapter 36

After Sam called 911, he sped back to the Quarter. He had left the phone containing Duval's confession atop Celeste's crude coffin, but the one thing he couldn't leave behind was his overwhelming sense of sorrow.

He had managed to get a full confession out of Duval before the cop fell unconscious. He knew NOPD would get the names and details out of him later.

After making sure Ramona was stable, Sam had made the call for assistance. He then pulled his car out of sight behind a hedge row and waited for the paramedics to show up. Once he knew help had arrived, he slipped away quietly down a deserted road that connected to the highway back to New Orleans.

Sam needed to speak with Maire. Alone. Too much had passed between them for him to leave town without telling her goodbye. She had been caring for Beatrice, and what few possessions he had were stored at her place. It had been his temporary home, and now he felt a deep sadness about leaving the city. When he thought about it, he realized that Maire's Gentleman's Club had been his go-to place since he was a lost teenager. Sometimes he still felt like a teenager when he was around Maire, but he understood now that she had been one of his last links with the past. He had come back to say goodbye to more people than he had realized. Sam wasn't sure where he would go. He just knew what no longer was.

After he pulled up to the Gentleman's club, he sat for a while and stared at the house, an old habit of his that had never died. The house had been a refuge for him—a place where he never felt lonely. But today, Sam felt as lonely as he had the day Kira died.

After Sam entered, one of the new girls told him Maire was still out and sent him up to her room to wait. "I know who you are," she said, "everyone knows Sam Lerner."

"Everyone except me," he thought to himself.

After he greeted Beatrice, he gave her some water and then shuffled around Maire's suite awhile. Everything about the room was feminine, from the silk damask coverlet on the dresser to the matching pillows. He would miss it.

His head still hurt so much it was hard to remain upright, so he lay on the bed until the buzzing in his ears subsided. He had been dozing for a few minutes when he heard Beatrice's tail thumping once again. He rolled onto his side as a familiar pair of long legs filled his field of vision. "Damn how I'd like to have those kickers wrapped around me," he drawled, letting his eyes sweep upward over her sensuous body to her exotic face.

"Well just let me slip out of this and let's see about that, chere," she smiled.

"Aw darlin', you know that's not going to happen. That time has long gone by."

Maire hesitated, looking down at him curiously. She took her time before speaking. He could sense she was finding her bearings. His dismissive response had thrown her off and now she was gauging her reaction very carefully. "Would you like to go hear some Jazz over on Frenchmen Street, or maybe have dinner first, Sam? Why don't we stop by Galatoire's for a bite?"

"I've have no appetite, Maire. I've been wallowing in a lot of shit. This afternoon I uncovered Duval's dirty extracurricular business. He was helping some ex-con kidnap your girls and fake their deaths so he could traffic them. I shot him, but I got a confession out of him before he became unconscious, so it won't matter now if he lives or dies."

Maire seemed to go limp as she dropped into a chair. "Oh my," she whispered, "Leon Duval?"

"Yes – and some sadist named Louis Santos. Apparently Santos had come around here a few times – maybe you remember him? Or have a record of him?"

"It would be impossible to say, chere. I run a business, but understandably, I keep few things on paper. We get one-time visitors and a whole assortment of regulars. Many make the rounds with different girls, so I can't help you there. What happened to that girl had nothing to do with us."

"It had to do with *somebody*. Think hard, sweetheart. You don't remember a guy who liked to rough girls up? He was mostly interested in Celeste."

"Yes, maybe I do remember him. If it's the same guy, I made him stop coming around because I feared he would hurt someone."

"Well he did. Celeste is dead, Maire. And Madsen's death was faked. She was never in that tomb you paid for."

"Oh god Sam, this just can't be true."

"Oh, but it can be. And you know that don't you?"

"What are you saying?"

"You know what I'm saying. Leon Duval was too stupid to be the brains behind this operation. So was his slimy friend Santos. Duval wasn't charging you protection when he came around here. He was delivering your cut of the action, wasn't he?"

"He told you that?"

"No." The change in Maire's breathing was almost imperceptible, but her look of relief did not go unnoticed by Sam. "But he didn't need to tell me."

"Chere, you've been through a lot. With that concussion you're not thinking straight." She lifted her long frame out of the rocker and moved gracefully toward the dresser. "I'm so hurt by your accusations I don't know what to think or say." She slid her hand across the top of the dresser as if to smooth the damask coverlet.

"Is this what you're looking for darlin'?" he asked holding up a silver pendant. Madsen's necklace still smelled of gardenia, although the piece of jewelry was tarnished in the few spots where the cheap silver plate still remained. It filled Sam with sorrow to look at it. "It was there on your dresser." Maire put her hand to her chest and gasped. "Sam, I don't know where that came from. I didn't even know she had a necklace like that."

"Yes you did. And you got it from Santos, didn't you? This was your proof that Madsen had been disposed of like some unwanted piece of garbage."

"You're wrong! Maybe someone here is trying to set me up."

"Really? Why is it that just now when I told you Madsen's death was a hoax you didn't even ask me where she is or if she's okay? I'll tell you why, love–it's because you already know. You were part of the cover up. Duval reported back to you on everything."

"That's absurd!"

"Bullshit! You sent him out to Bayou LaFourche the day Charlie died. He was going to dispose of Charlie. And then he was going to take care of me, wasn't he? Duval was the one who tried to push me off the road when we left Cat's Blues Heaven."

"You're confused, chere. It was too dark to see.

"I may not have seen who rammed me that night, but I can recognize a god-damn police car engine when I hear one."

"Sam, think about what you're saying. Why would I have gone out there to meet you if I thought Leon Duval was going to "take care of you" as you so delicately put it? I came because I thought you needed me."

"No darlin, when you heard from Duval that Charlie was already dead and Duval had missed us both, you needed to know if Charlie had told me his suspicions about your little enterprise before saying his final farewell. That night at Cat's, you said Jem had told you Charlie died. But I never told her he died, Maire. We lost the connection before I could give her the news. I knew you were lying then, but I needed time to figure out why."

Maire smiled oddly, then with one sudden movement, she yanked open the drawer of her dresser and thrust her hand inside. Sam sat in silence, watching as her shoulders caved in with defeat.

"Sorry darlin' but it's not there." Sam reached under the pillow and held up a firearm. "We're you actually going to shoot your old love?"

Maire's face was ashen as she dropped back into the chair, her long legs no longer able to support her bodyweight. They sat in silence for several moments while all their endings gathered round them like sad ghosts.

"No one was going to miss them," Maire finally whispered. "They would be doing the same thing in Cuba they were doing here, and we would all make some money for providing a service. That's what I have always done Sam, I provide a service. They were professional call girls. They sold themselves. But maybe you see me the same way. Do you?"

"No, I never saw you that way, Maire, but now I realize I never really saw you at all."

"You don't understand."

"Oh, but I think I do."

"Well I didn't sell myself like the girls in my charge—that must count for something. I slept with you because we have been part of each other's lives for almost three decades. You know we never really left each other. You're different than the rest, chere."

"Well let's not forget Santos. You slept with him, didn't you? That's how you got him to do what you wanted."

"Sam-"

"When I was last here, I spotted a tip of an Esplendido over there in your trash can, but it took me some time to put it altogether. I guess I wanted to believe in us– you and me –just a little bit longer. You thought you could control him better than Celeste could, but in the end, sweetheart, he was the one using you."

"Sam, I made a horrible mistake, I know that. I just needed some money so I could quit this business and get out of the Quarter. I have a place down in Martinique. Come with me."

"You know that can't happen."

"Please. Everyone deserves a second chance. Let's do it together. I know you don't have any other place to go."

"You're wrong. I have plenty of places I can go, just no place to go back to. I wanted that place to be you, but you were always a fantasy." Sam sighed and shook his head when he noticed Maire crying softly. "It's odd, but when Duval confessed, he gave me names, but he never mentioned you. You're the one person he is protecting and probably will continue to cover for you. He has always had a distorted sense of gentlemen's honor."

"But you don't?"

"No darlin', I'm afraid I don't".

"Please, Sam. If no one knows of my involvement, then you can let me go, can't you? I could never survive in prison. Oh Jesus, Sam – please! Let's spend the last years of our lives making love under the Caribbean sun. We can put this behind us."

"Stop, Maire. It's over. I called in a report on my way over here."

Maire looked as if she had been slapped. "Why would you do that? Why Sam? You know I have always loved you."

"No darling, what I discovered is that *I* always loved *you*. And this is just one more shitty goodbye." When he rose to leave, Maire suddenly threw herself at him, grappling for the gun. He yanked his arm away and held the gun just out of her reach as his gaze lingered on the face that was as familiar to him as his own.

Sam ran a finger across her cheek. Maire would always be beautiful to him. She was a piece of his past he hadn't been able to let go of. But he couldn't carry that past around with him anymore.

After a beat, Sam thrust the firearm at her. "You want to do it, love?" he asked "Then just do it. You already took the last of me."

Startled by his gesture, Maire took a step back. Then she grabbed the gun, pausing only a moment before pressing it to his chest. Sam didn't flinch as he signaled Beatrice to remain in place. Maire smiled sadly just before she cocked the gun. "Chere, you always gave me too much credit. Too many years have gone by. Life got real dark for me. But there were moments between us when I thought maybe I could fix things…maybe have a new life with you. But we both knew those moments weren't real, didn't we, Sam?"

"I suppose. But maybe I was the last to figure it out. I knew you well, love. I just didn't know all of you. I do know one thing, however…you aren't going to shoot me."

"Are you sure?"

"I'm your last connection to the good person you once were. If you kill me, we both die. And I'm willing to gamble that you won't do that."

Sam nodded as if to say a final goodbye. He brushed his hand against her arm as he walked past her toward the door. "Chere," she whispered to his back.

Sam winced when he heard the gun shot. He turned around slowly, already knowing what to expect. His last view of Maire lying dead on the floor was more painful than he could ever have imagined.

Epilogue

The drive out of New Orleans was as beautiful as when he had first come back, but even the Cajun music on the radio could barely lift his spirits. He had hoped his return to the French Quarter would bring him comfort, but he had been running from a sorrow that had consumed his life.

He would visit again next year to check on Jem, and maybe even drop by the Zydeco Festival, but now he was heading back to Los Angeles in hopes of sloughing off the decay of something far darker than anything he could ever have imagined. Sam knew that eventually he would find happiness again, but he would never forget. He clung to the words Renee Oleyant had told him when he bid his final farewell: "We honor the dead by remembering, not by forgetting."

He had loved two women, each differently—one good, and one who had lost her way. And now they both were dead. No, there was no forgetting. "Rest in Peace, chere," he whispered as he stepped on the accelerator. Beatrice, as content as always just to be along for the ride, settled into the seat next to him while Sam turned up the volume and sucked in the warm air of Lake Ponchartrain.

Acknowledgements

It has always been interesting to me that although authors string words together into thought, it is often so difficult for us to find a way to express our true appreciation to those whose support has made an endeavor possible. Thus, I will simply offer a sincere thank you and hope that those words will reflect the never-ending gratitude I have for the encouragement from the following people:

Antony Bland, Jan Pastras and Craig Nadeau for being the first independent "eyes" to help guide and encourage publication of this book. Dr. Dmitry Arbuck, who never lets me forget I am a writer. Buddy, who keeps me company when I burn the midnight oil. My publisher, Creativia, and specifically Miika Hannila for believing my work is worth the time and investment. And of course to my family who always express the pride that motivates me and the love that sustains me.

Gwen Banta
Los Angeles, 2018

About the Author

Gwen Banta was born in New York and received B.A. and M.S. degrees from Butler University. She has received numerous accolades for her fiction, including the Opus Magnum Discovery Award For New Literature and six Winner commendations for Unpublished Stories in book festivals throughout the U.S. and Europe.

A former award-winning actor of stage, screen and television, Gwen is a member of SAG/AFTRA and AEA and has also received numerous awards for her screenplays. Her screenplay, Skies A Fallin,' is currently under option. Gwen lives in Los Angeles with her dog, Buddy, who is a great fan of her work.